Paving Stones

Also by Edna Taylor and published by Ginninderra Press
Skeleton in the Cupboard
Brief Encounters
The Attic
The Empty Chair

Edna Taylor

Paving Stones

Paving Stones
ISBN 978 1 76041 103 2
Copyright © Edna Taylor 2021
Cover image: congerdesign on Pixabay

First published 2021 by
GINNINDERRA PRESS
PO Box 3461 Port Adelaide 5015
www.ginninderrapress.com.au

Contents

There be a Dragon

Dimas was sitting cross-legged on stop of the fridge. His eyes were wide open with fright and he scrunched as far back as he could into the corner against the wall. The fridge was quite large and his kitchen small, so there wasn't much room; luckily he was a small man and able to squeeze into tight spots.

The Komodo dragon had caught him unawares. It must, he thought, have followed him. Dimas had cycled home as usual from his job at the national park. He had seen plenty of dragons. They were protected, they were enormous, they were dangerous and they were meat-eaters, but they didn't often come near to homes and generally speaking Dimas wasn't scared of them. In fact, he admired and respected them, but he was always careful not to get too close to the big ones, always mindful that they are wild, ferocious and unpredictable.

He had lived on Komodo Island all of his life, twenty years, and the dragons lived in the park. He had watched their babies hatch out and seen them climb up into the trees until they were big enough to fend for themselves on the ground where they feasted on wild hogs and native animals.

It had started to rain heavily as Dimas had ridden home and he threw his bike down to the ground, ran up the steps to his door and rushed inside, put his bottle of water down, and pulled his phone out of his pocket. The battery was flat and he needed to be on call for work. So he went directly to the corner of the room and attached the phone to the lead plugged into the socket near the floor.

He hadn't bothered to close the door properly and it made him jump as it suddenly banged against the wall. Dimas had turned and then froze; the head of a large dragon was coming through his door followed by an enormous body and it was making the strange loud hissing noise dragons make when they're angry. There was a foul smell filling the room and the sight and sound was menacing enough to jolt Dimas out of his shock. He had to act fast.

He couldn't get out. There was only one outside door in his small house and now it was blocked, so he threw himself onto the small cupboard alongside the fridge and then pulled himself up onto the top, which was where he now sat, quivering, terrified and frozen with fear.

The dragon pulled itself into the room. Its tail flicked against the door again which banged shut. It turned around a couple of times as if checking out the room, its forked tongue flickering in and out smelling for food, and then settled its great body onto the floor and turned its head up towards Dimas, eyes glaring, mouth slightly open, and he could see the enormous teeth with bits of debris oozing out from between them.

They stared at one another. Dimas stopped shaking as he realised that for the time being he was safe. The dragon was about two metres long, including his enormous tail, so it couldn't reach the top of the fridge unless it stood on its hind legs and even then it couldn't reach far back enough to attack him. At least he hoped it couldn't.

Dimas looked over to his phone. He couldn't get to it, that was obvious, but maybe someone would ring him and when he didn't answer they would come to investigate. Then he realised. Today was Saturday. He had finished work for today, and tomorrow, being Sunday, was his day off. No one was likely to check unless there was an emergency; he was on standby call if this happened and then it was generally a tourist who had gone into the restricted area, got lost and panicked.

He tried to wriggle himself into a more comfortable position but as soon as it saw the movement, the dragon roused itself up, alert and carefully watching, so Dimas stayed still, and the dragon stayed still, eyes focused, waiting, ready to make its move.

Dimas tried to calm himself, to think. He looked over to the door and wondered whether he could jump over the reptile and get to the door before it had time to turn around. Its tail was against the door but if he could get it to shift, to turn around and put its tail somewhere else, then maybe it would work, but he had seen how quickly they could move, so it was too big a risk. Dimas looked at the window over the cupboard alongside the fridge. It hadn't been opened for a long time and was probably stuck; it would take too long and he would have to break the glass to get out.

He glanced at his watch. It would be dusk soon and he couldn't reach the light switch, so when night came it was going to be very dark. Dimas tried to still the panic rising in his chest, his heart raced and he was having trouble breathing. He tried not to look at the dragon and stop imagining what those teeth could do. He remembered the talk given to the staff at the park about the fact that toxic bacteria in the mouth of the dragon was no longer considered to be the cause of death, and that the dragons had venom in the gums between their teeth which oozed out into its prey after it had been bitten and ripped. It took effect slowly and rendered the victims powerless to move or fight back, so eventually they died. Sometimes it took up to three days and the dragon waited patiently, not moving, watching and sometimes, if it was hungry enough, it would start eating its victim before it was dead.

So Dimas tried not to think about all those things. Slowly he moved his legs around so that his knees were folded up to his chest and he rested his head on top. He closed his eyes and thought about how hungry he was feeling. There was a small gas stove with two burners resting on a low table in the opposite corner across the room with a gas bottle alongside. There was a cooking pot on the top waiting for some rice and vegetables which he put into the fridge yesterday.

He opened his eyes and thought about the fridge. There was a handle which had to be moved downward to open the door, so he couldn't open it even if he managed to lean over far enough. So that wouldn't work.

He sighed. He eyed the cupboard. His bottle of water was on the top where he had put it when he had come home. He looked at the dragon, which hadn't moved, and made a plan: as soon as it got dark, which wouldn't be long now, he would get his water. He thought he could lean over far enough to reach the top of the cupboard and grab the bottle before the big lizard could react. He hoped dragons couldn't see in the dark.

Thinking about the water made Dimas want to pee. He was fastidious. His small two-roomed wooden house was always spotless. There was no inside toilet, just the outside longdrop, and the thought of having to make water over the side of the fridge onto his nice clean floor was almost more than he could bear, but there was no option.

So as quietly and quickly as he could, Dimas undid his pants and dribbled over the side of the fridge nearest the wall, watching the dragon all the time. Its tongue flicked in and out, smelling something different. It hissed, but didn't move from its place on the floor.

Dragons generally rest during the heat of the day and go hunting in the cool of the evening. Dimas was thinking that maybe it would try and get out now, but he looked over towards the door where the great tail was still wedged and realised; it was trapped inside. They were both trapped inside!

Suddenly, the dragon raised himself up and started prowling around. It banged its head against the door, and the walls, hissing, tongue flicking in and out. Dimas's cooking pot landed on the floor and his stool went flying across the room. Heart thumping, he drew himself as close to the wall as he could get. It was dark now. moonlight was shining through the little window, and he could see that that the dragon was getting angrier. Then it seemed to tire and stopped moving; it looked around and, as if realising it was trapped, it sank back again onto the floor.

Dimas looked down for a moment and saw a reflection from the moonlight trapped in the lizard's eyes. It sent a shiver up his spine and it seemed as though the devil himself was watching and waiting for him. He prayed that it couldn't see him in his dark corner on top of the fridge.

All was quiet again now and Dimas settled as comfortably as he could and then waited and waited for a long time, and then he was getting so thirsty, he decided to take a chance. He couldn't tell if the dragon was asleep or not but, holding his breath and little by little, he edged himself over to the side of the fridge, spread out onto his stomach and leaned over, just managing to grab his water and get back up again.

He was quick but the dragon sensed the movement and was immediately up on its feet, searching for him as Dimas drew himself back into his corner.

That night was probably the worst of Dimas's life. He dozed on and off, sipping his water to make it last. The smell from the dragon was worse than ever and he realised that it had probably defecated onto the floor.

A couple of times during the night it got up and crawled around and then settled again. It was very dark now, the moon had gone and Dimas couldn't see whether the dragon's tail was still wedged against the door. He thought again about trying to make a run for it but his gut was telling him not to take the risk; he could trip, he wouldn't stand a chance if it attacked.

He thought about getting to his sleeping space. The door to this room was facing him, only about four metres away, and he knew that the window in there was always a little bit open. He wondered if he could get across quickly enough and have time to shut the door then climb out through the other window. Dimas wished he had more courage. His thoughts became dark with despair. He could die this night right here in his own kitchen. He dare not sleep. If his leg slipped over the edge of the fridge, the dragon could pull him off.

He was so tired now and tears oozed out from behind heavy eyelids as Dimas thought about Indah, the new girl in the ranger's office. Yesterday she had smiled at him, really noticed him for the first time. He had been trying to get up the courage to ask her out for weeks and now he might never get the chance!

What if nobody came! What if he wasn't even missed! They might think he'd gone away and give his job to somebody else. He would soon be a qualified ranger; it was his goal and he had worked hard, learning as much as he could. Even his English was getting better so that he could talk to the tourists. Would it all be for nothing?

It was almost dawn before Dimas finally dozed off but the cramp in his legs grabbed him as he shifted again and he opened his eyes to see the dragon, still in the same position, watching him.

Light was beginning to brighten the room when the jangle of the phone pierced the quiet stillness and the dragon jumped, alert, looking around.

Dimas almost wept then. He listened to the phone ring itself out and his answering machine kicked in. 'This is Dimas. I am busy. Please call back.' Someone will come now, he thought; they will check.

Ten minutes later, the phone rang again. 'Please come,' he whispered. 'Please come!'

Another long ten minutes passed, then there was the sound of a motor engine stopping outside and a car door slamming. The loud knocking on the outside door startled the dragon, it jumped up and charged towards it, hissing, its tongue flickering, and then there was the welcome sound of Dimas's friend Ketut's voice.

'Open the door, Dimas. Are you OK?' He was trying to open the door, which now had the dragon's head banging against it. 'The door's stuck! What's going on? Dimas?'

'There's a dragon in here,' Dimas shouted. 'It's blocking the door!'

'Did you say a dragon?' Ketut sounded disbelieving.

'Yes, and I can't get out.'

He heard footsteps going around the house and then looked down to see the face of his friend peering through the window. Eyes like saucers. 'Where are you?' he shouted. 'I can't see you!'

'On the fridge!'

'How long you been there?'

'All night!'

'All night?'

'Yes.'

'How you going to get out?'

'I don't know.'

There was silence as Ketut disappeared for a couple of minutes then he came back. 'I have idea.'

'Yes?

'Yes. I climb through other window and open other door and make noise and when dragon turn round to see me you run to front door and get out. Little problem, though.'

'What problem?'

'Window not open much. I have to break glass to get in.'

Dimas pondered on this for a moment. 'Break glass doesn't matter. But if he see you, he can move quick and then you are caput, Ketut!'

'I am quick also. I shut the door, he can't get me.'

Dimas was now desperate to pee again and was willing to try anything. The dragon was getting restless. Its great feet were stomping on the floor, he was turning round and round then charging against the wall. He was a fearsome sight. Tail swinging, hissing away, and the house was shaking.

'OK,' Dimas shouted. 'We do this. I am ready. When you ready, you bang hard.'

He waited. Heart thumping, adrenalin coursing through his body. Then a sound of smashing glass, followed a moment later with a thump on the door.

'You ready?' Ketut shouted.

'Yes, ready.' Dimas was up on his knees now as the dragon turned its attention to the other door. He got ready to jump down onto the cupboard before reaching the floor, hoping his legs wouldn't give way after not being able to stretch for so long.

The door opened slowly and Ketut peered in, eyes widening with horror as the dragon turned towards him and started to charge. He closed it again quickly, but Dimas was flying. He jumped down behind the dragon and was at the front door in two seconds He flung it open and ran round to the side of the house to meet Ketut. They hugged for a moment, then watched, ready to make a run for it. But they needn't have worried. The dragon had made his escape through the now open front door without a backward glance and headed straight for the trees and its hideout, where no doubt he rested during the heat of the day.

'You OK?' Ketut regarded his friend with something like awe. 'You stayed there all night? Were you scared?'

'Yes, a little bit,' confessed Dimas.

They walked back into the house, where Dimas surveyed with disgust his kitchen floor and the rug where he sat to eat his food. 'Big mess!' He dragged the rug outside and attached a water hose to a tap. 'I'll have to clean everything now.'

He turned to Ketut, who was fingering his car keys and regarding him anxiously.

'It's OK now. I'm OK now,' Dimas reassured him. 'Thank you, Ketut. You saved my life.'

Now that it was all over, he felt so overwhelmed he wanted to weep, but he didn't want Ketut to see how really shaken up he was. He had to be strong to work with dragons. He didn't want to appear to be weak. He felt a little bit proud as well. He had survived the night and he felt he had the courage to do anything now. Then he had a thought.

'Why did you come, Ketut? Why did you phone me?'

'Oh,' Ketut smiled. 'Stupid tourist left gate open and dragon chased him from restricted area, then disappeared. I came to get you to help find dragon and take him back.' He patted Dimas on the back. 'Now no need. I'll tell boss Dimas found him. Maybe you'll get pay rise!' He laughed and waved goodbye as he climbed into the truck.

Dimas waved back then quickly headed for the long-drop.

Poker Machine

'What's Charley building in his backyard?' George asked Harry when they were having their usual in the local pub.

'Dunno. Looks like another room.'

'Why would he need another room?' George looked puzzled. 'There's only him living there.'

'P'raps it's for an outside dunny.'

'Naa, shouldn't think so. What's the point of that?'

So they pondered and speculated. The two mates lived either side of Charley's place and the fences between the backyards were low enough so that you didn't have to stretch much to see what the neighbours were up to and the next time George was outside and heard Charley working over there, he peered over the top.

'What ya doing then, Charley?' he called.

Charley put down the brick he was holding and held up a trowel filled with concrete mix. 'Hi, George,' he smiled. It was hard to see Charley smile because his enormous moustache drooped over his mouth and you never knew quite knew what he was thinking, but though his eyes smiled, he always looked as if he was hiding a secret. 'It's just a shed,' he said now and turned back to his bricklaying.

'What's it for then?'

This time Charley didn't turn round. 'I'll tell you when it's ready,' he said, and George had no option but to leave it at that.

'He's building a shed?' Harry asked in surprise after George told him. What's he going to put in another shed? He's already got a shed. Admitted, it looks a bit worse for wear, but nothing that a coat of paint wouldn't fix up.'

'He said he'd tell me when it's ready,' George told him when they were again pondering on the strangeness of their neighbour's doings. 'It must be a secret.'

'He always was a bit strange,' remarked Harry, 'always inventing stuff. It must be a Pommy thing. Remember when he made that contraption that was supposed to be a spinning watchamacallit for dice that kept sticking in one place and the same numbers came up every time?'

'Yeah, and thing that looked like an upmarket abacus. I never knew what he intended to do with that.'

They laughed, sipped their beer and talked about other things. But George was wasn't giving up easily and every time he went into the backyard, he carefully peered over the fence. He didn't want Charley to think he was spying, so to speak, so he kept quiet and watched as the shed gradually took shape; about three metres square, he reckoned. Then one day a couple of blokes came and put on the roof, a nice heritage green and, another time, a solid wooden door was attached.

George was woken up around midnight on a couple of occasions after that when he heard Charley's old ute drive in to his garage next door, and he wondered where he had been, considering his neighbour rarely went out socialising, but he didn't associate it with the happenings in the shed.

George's wife Betty wondered what he was doing spending so much time in the backyard. 'What ya doing out there then?' she finally asked him one day.

'Just watching him next door,' he told her. 'He's building a shed. Wondering what it's for.'

'Well, that's his business, isn't it? When are you going to get going on that vegie patch like you've been thinking about?'

'I am,' he said. 'I'm just waiting on some topsoil.' George was not an enthusiastic gardener.

Nothing much happened for about a week after that, then one day a truck arrived and George peeked over the fence to see what was happening. He couldn't see much, though, just a big crate which seemed to be very heavy, as it took two big blokes to lift it and carry it through into the shed, then they left. Shortly after that, another bloke came in an electrician's van and fixed up some wiring connections from the house to the shed. All very exciting it was, as George related to Harry in the pub later.

'Whatever he's got in there, it makes a lot of racket,' said George. 'Like a grating, whirring sound, and a high-pitched whistling. I watched him come out yesterday. He'd been in there for hours, it seemed, and he fairly staggered into the house. Makes you wonder, don' it?'

'Well, I reckon he's invented something,' Harry said. 'No doubt he'll tell us when he's ready.'

They didn't have to wait long. A few days later, a note appeared in both their letter boxes. 'You are invited to the grand opening of the Charley Baker Poker Machine next Saturday at 2 o'clock,' it said.

George and Harry could scarcely contain themselves.

'We'll have to take a few cans,' said Harry. 'Can't go empty-handed.'

'And some small change,' added George. 'I wonder if it's for twenty cents? Or maybe a dollar and two-dollar coins. We'd better take some of each to be on the safe side. That wily old bugger,' he laughed, 'fancy that. All this time, he's been building a poker machine,'

So the following Saturday they both turned up on time with a carton of beer plus loose change jangling in their pockets. Charley was waiting for them outside the shed. He had put some garden chairs around a table on the grass under an umbrella.

'G'day, George, and you too, Harry.' He eyed the carton of beer which Harry had put down and shook both their hands.

Always polite was Charley, thought George, as their host said, 'Thank you for coming, and thank you for the beer. That's very kind of you.'

'No worries,' said Harry, 'and thanks for inviting us.' He eyed the closed door of the shed. 'So you've invented a poker machine then?'

'Yes, I'll show it to you in a minute. It's got to get warmed up for a bit before it'll work.' He looked at his watch. 'Perhaps we could have a beer first?' He picked up a can and proceeded to open it.

The others nodded and did the same.

'Cheers,' said George. 'Here's to the success of Charley's poker machine.'

They all clinked cans and sipped and listened to a whirring sound coming from the shed, and trying to find something to talk about, until George ,who could scarcely contain himself, said hopefully, 'Is it ready yet then?'

Charley nodded. 'Should be OK now.'

He got up from his chair and they followed him to the door, which had been padlocked, then waited while Charley opened it up and they all peered into the dimly lit shed. There was a small window which gave some light, but a power point had been installed, which Charley switched on, then looked proudly at his contraption.

George and Harry could say nothing at first. They regarded the machine with awe. Wheels were spinning, pistons were going up and down, a piece of metal was being banged about and turned around and hammered and they watched, transfixed, as it finally plummeted out and landed in a receptacle where there were similar-looking objects.

Charley picked one of them up and handed it to George, who held the thing and peered at it, moving it from one hand to the other. 'It's a bit hot,' he said.

'Yes, they are a bit hot when they come out,' said Charley. 'It'll cool down fairly quickly,'

'But what is it?' asked George finally, totally confused. 'I thought you said it was a poker machine.'

Harry couldn't speak. He was still gazing transfixed at the amazing contraption which was still clanging away.

'Yes, that's right, a poker machine,' Charley said patiently. 'A machine for making pokers.'

'Oh,' George looked at the poker in his hand and wielded it around the air like a sword. 'Well, OK then, what would you do with a poker?'

'Poke things of course.'

'Like what?' George couldn't help sounding a little sceptical.

'Like fires for one thing. Everybody needs a poker for a fire.'

'I don't have a fireplace. I'm all electrical.'

Charley looked puzzled. 'I thought everyone had a fireplace. I have a fireplace.'

Harry had picked one of the pokers up. 'I think they're beaut,' he said. He held it up. 'You could have your name engraved on it, then nobody would nick it.' He reached for his glasses in his top pocket to have a closer look. Indeed, he thought, it was a fine-looking poker. There was a point at one end and the handle part had been flattened out and slightly bent, making it comfortable to hold. This one was painted green, although the paint looked quite old. Harry glanced to the corner of the room, where there appeared to be a pile of old iron fence railings. He glanced at Charley, who was looking so pleased with himself that he bit back what he was about to say.

George was thinking aloud. 'Well, I s'pose it would be good for making holes in the ground for planting seeds and stuff,' he said.

'Yeah,' said Harry, and it'd be handy if someone tried to break into your place. A clout across the skull with this would do a bit of damage.' He waved the poker around in the air and laughed then quietened as he looked out of the half opened door. 'Whoops!' he said.

'What is it?' Charley asked him, and they all stepped outside.

A small queue was forming by the back gate.

'Looks like word's got around,' said George, realising that Betty had probably seen the invite and couldn't resist telling her friends.

'Let them in,' Charley smiled. 'I think I have enough made for everybody.'

'How much are they?' George wanted to know.

'Ten dollars, I reckon,' said Harry, and eyes raised in question, turned to Charley, who nodded.

Harry emptied out his pockets. 'There you go then, Charley, ten bucks. I'll be your first customer.'

The Wolf

The old grey wolf padded silently through the forest. He hadn't seen a human for a long time. He stayed away from them; he knew they would hunt him down. If he saw one, he kept himself hidden.

The wolf hunted deer and other wild life when he was hungry, and fended for himself. There was no need for territory fights any more; the rest of his pack were gone and he was alone now. The hunters had left without spotting the big grey wolf, so the forest had been quiet for a long time, until today.

He had seen the human, a young one. He was collecting wood to make a fire and the wolf had smelled the rabbit. He often killed rabbits nowadays; they were easier than the deer. He was old and it was getting harder for him to hunt; his legs didn't run as fast as they used to and he tired quickly,

The wolf stopped and stood very still. He watched as the boy skilfully skinned and gutted one of the rabbits, then lay it down on top of a tree stump. Next, he opened up a backpack and spread out a sleeping bag onto the ground.

The wolf crouched down and waited, moving his head slightly, looking to see if there was a gun, ready to run, but there was no sign of any weapon and the wolf relaxed slightly. but he was hungry; he hadn't been able to hunt down anything today.

The boy started the fire now and as he turned to pick up more wood, he thought he saw out of the corner of his eye a small movement. He stopped what he was doing and stayed quite still, listening for a long moment, but he neither heard nor saw anything, so shrugged and then carried on with his fire until it was burning brightly. Next, he selected two strong forked sticks and stuck them into the ground, then, using another one, he made a rough spit, carefully drove it through the skinned rabbit and suspended it above the fire. The boy sat down on his sleeping bag and, pulling a harmonica out of his pants pocket, he began to play.

The wolf crept closer and the boy suddenly stopped playing. He sat quite still again listening; only his eyes moved, settling on a nearby bush, and he knew.

'I know you're there,' he said, his voice trembling just a little bit.

The wolf emerged from behind the bush. He felt no fear now; the voice was soft, not hard and menacing like the hunters.

The boy watched him warily but felt no threat. 'Are you hungry?' he said. 'I bet you like rabbit.' He held the other unskinned rabbit up.

The wolf came closer now, still a little cautious but with growing confidence. He stopped and proudly drew himself up to his full height, looking down at the boy. For a long moment, they locked eyes. There was an understanding, a meeting of souls recognising in that brief moment a kinship, a mutual respect and understanding, then the wolf gently wrapped his jaw around the rabbit, turned and quickly disappeared back into the forest.

The boy let out a long breath. 'Awesome!' he muttered, then turned as a man holding a rifle appeared from the opposite direction.

'Good boy,' he said. 'You've got the fire going then.' He waved the gun around. 'Don't think we'll need this, but I've got it just in case. there are no sounds or signs of any wolves around here, but you never know.' He looked at the rabbit cooking over the fire. 'What happened to the other one?' he asked.

The boy eyed the gun then turned his head back to look into the fire. 'The other one was all mangled and smelt funny,' he said, 'so I chucked it away.'

Litterbugs

The drones were out in force that day. They were the latest money-making scheme devised by the local council, who were not making enough income from speeding fines any more. People drove more carefully these days, heeding road signs, wearing seatbelts and so on. They had become smart at spotting cop cars as well, even unmarked ones. Pedestrians also were more careful now after the heavy fines imposed for loitering, or not using pedestrian crossings.

Hence the drones. For littering, no less. They – the litter drones, that is – were equipped with powerful magnifiers that could zone in on the smallest object that some unwitting person had aimlessly chucked onto the ground. Mind you, it must have cost a whole heap of money to buy the drones in the first place, by a council that was supposed to be short of money; so go figure.

Anyway, I was sitting outside the local café with a cup of coffee and watching an approaching drone, which stopped right over the park up to the north of town.

They were inclined to get in position high above where they were patrolling, and then drop like a spider attached to its web and just dangle or hover over some unsuspecting miscreant. I watched it drop and then heard the menacing booming voice coming from the drone. 'Pick up your litter! You have thirty seconds!'

I could imagine the people there rushing to dispose of anything they might have disregarded. Could be a child dropping a drink box or perhaps the dog had done a poo which you hadn't noticed, or perhaps you had forgotten to bring the doggie poo bag, in which case you could be in a whole heap of trouble.

Unfortunately, there were no excuses accepted. Children were supposed to be controlled by the adults. Also, because there were face recognition devises attached to the drones, no one could escape, and I could imagine those people over at the park scrambling to find a litter bin, which were all over the place around town so it was always best to be in the vicinity of one just in case. Penalties were harsh. If you hadn't disposed of your litter in thirty seconds, the police patrol, which were always lurking around, would turn up and then you were nabbed.

Fines were given according to the size of the litter. Cigarette butts were $100 and a drink carton about $200. If the fine wasn't paid within a month, then the offender would be sent off to the littering prison farm to do community service, where all the garbage collected in bins around town would be tipped out onto the exercise yard and prisoners had to pick it all up again and replace it in other bins. which were eventually taken to the dump.

First offenders might only do this for a week. But repeat offenders were treated more harshly. Sometimes they disappeared for a month. This was supposed to teach people a lesson not to litter. I don't know if it worked. I've never been caught, I'm glad to say, but I bet those who have were not likely to litter again.

Anyway, the drone over the park started coming towards the main street and people were looking around, anxiously making sure there was no rubbish lying about. Then I noticed old Bertie coming out of the pub across the road. He was lighting up a smoke. Cigarettes were still not banned – let's face it, the government still got revenue from the sale of them – but you were not allowed to smoke in public places, so old Bertie should have been more careful. He hadn't noticed the drone which was now hovering overhead until just at the last minute as it swooped down. He looked up, panicked and chucked his lit cigarette into the trash bin alongside the pub door. Next thing, smoke started pouring out of the bin. A police car came hurtling around the corner and I heard someone in the café loudly phoning the fire station, which luckily was not too far away.

Meanwhile, the drone, which had started booming, 'Pick up your litter! 'suddenly stopped mid-sentence, as Bertie's cigarette had disappeared in about ten seconds. Unfortunately for him, though, a policeman was bringing out some handcuffs. I have no idea what the penalty would be for starting a fire. No doubt, old Bertie found out soon enough. We haven't seen him since, and that was about four weeks ago.

Anyway, next thing, another drone started hovering around, probably backup for the other one, which had started to take off again, but someone in the control room, or whoever is monitoring these things, must have got confused or something, because just as the first drone started to go up, the second one came down and, well, they collided, didn't they, and they both fell in a great big heap in the middle of the high street. In bits.

Next thing, the fire engine came round the corner and almost ran over the crashed drones, but the firies weren't really needed by then because the pub owner had come out with a bucket of water and doused the fire burning away in the bin. They looked quite disappointed; there wasn't much call for a fire engine these days, so they didn't get much practice. I can't remember the last time there was a fire.

By now, there was a great crowd of gawping onlookers gazing upwards and looking at yet another drone approaching at speed, at ground level this time. It stopped and hovered over the crashed drones and then a great booming voice called out, 'Pick up your litter! You have thirty seconds.'

Nobody moved. After all, it wasn't our litter, was it? It was the council's and it was their job to clean up their own mess, which they did eventually. It took two days, though, and we had to divert traffic away from the main street until it was done. Funnily enough, we haven't seen any more litter drones since then. I reckon the council has run out of money.

So things are getting back to normal. Plus – and this was a big surprise – our town got the Tidiest Town award for this year.

Go figure!

The Path

The path was not on the map. It led away from the highway and there was an old-fashioned stile just asking to be climbed over. Shrubs and weeds almost covered it and if we hadn't stopped for Gazza to take a leak, then we probably wouldn't have noticed it at all.

The car was parked on the verge and not in the way of traffic, so when Simon said, 'I wonder where that goes to then?' we all climbed out to have a better look.

'Well, who's game then?' Gazza was already pushing stuff aside and starting to climb over, so from force of habit and doing whatever Gazza said, me and Mikey and Simon climbed over as well.

'Did you remember to lock the car, Gazza?' I asked, and he nodded, 'Yeah, 'course I did.'

It always seemed to be me who did the reminding for stuff like that. Gazza liked to think he was in charge, and he was, so long as other people reminded him about things sometimes. Anyway, that's beside the point. We started up the path. It wasn't much of a path really, just a track almost covered over with weeds and stuff falling on it from the trees overhead. It was like a mini forest and the further we went in, the darker it got.

'I think we've gone far enough.' Simon was always a bit of a worrier. 'I can't even see the car any more,' he said. 'Suppose someone nicked it. We got all our gear in there.'

'I just wanna see where this goes to.' Gazza sounded confident. He always did, so everyone always went along with him.

So anyway, we kept walking and there was nothing, not even a sign of a house or anything except more and more bushes and scrub, and we had to keep pushing stuff out of the way. We were getting scratched and my leg was bleeding from where a jagged branch had stuck into it.

I stopped walking then. 'OK,' I said, 'that's it. I'm done. This is a waste of time.' I looked around. 'This doesn't go anywhere. It's probably just an animal track that might end up with some water but that could be ks away.' I suddenly realised something. 'Where's Mikey?' I said.

The others stopped and looked around.

'I thought he was behind me,' said Simon.

'Mikey,' I called out then, and Gazza and Simon did as well.

We all turned around and walked back for a bit, still calling out, but when we stopped to listen there wasn't a sound. I realised then that it was uncannily quiet. I mean, there were no birds, no breeze, no leaves rustling, no nothing, just quiet.

'Come on. We better go back. Maybe he went for a leak and got lost, or maybe he didn't hear us. He can't be far.' Gazza was sounding confident as he turned round and started walking purposefully back along the path, which was a bit easier to follow now that we had cleared some of the stuff away.

So we called and called, and I was getting worried now, I have to admit. It was dusk, it would be getting dark soon and the trees seemed to be closing in on us. The path was getting harder to see, so we kept close behind Gazza, but when he suddenly turned and started walking along another rough track off to the side, I stopped. So did Simon.

'Come on,' said Gazza. 'What have you stopped for? He might have gone this way. We might as well check it out. We'll go along here for a bit and see.'

So we traipsed behind for a little way until I realised that the track had disappeared, and suddenly Gazza halted.

'I think we're lost,' he said. He didn't sound so confident now and turned to me. 'What d'you reckon, Jen?'

Now, to say this was unusual was to say the least. I'm Jenna, Gazza's sister. I'm a year younger than him, he just got his driving licence and I can't wait to get mine. Anyway, the thing is, he never asks my opinion about anything. He tolerates my keyboard-playing in our little band mainly because he can't find anyone else, although personally I think I am as good as he is going to get. He plays guitar and Mikey and Simon, who are both fourteen, are learning to play drums and bass, which is why we were going to Jack's place for a bit of a practice, seeing as it was Saturday. We were early. At least, we were early until we had to stop for my brother, who never thinks to go the loo before we leave to go anywhere. Anyway, that's all beside the point. The thing is that now we were going to be very late and Jack will probably think we're a bunch of losers.

I peered at my watch. 'It's stopped,' I said. which was strange because it had never stopped before, just for no reason. I knew it wasn't the battery. I had only replaced it a couple of weeks ago. 'What about your phone, Gazza?' I asked him. 'We can call Mikey and he can tell us where he is. He always carries his phone.'

Gazza looked a bit sheepish, which was also very unusual for him. 'Didn't bring it, did I,' he said. 'It was on the charger.'

I looked at Simon, who shook his head. 'Nah, didn't bring it,' he said.

So I heaved the backpack off my back and delved in, looking for my phone. Found it and then discovered to my disbelief there was no signal. 'No signal,' I said.

For a long moment, we stood and looked at one another. I tried to think of what to do next. We had lost Mikey, we had no contact with anybody. Our families would think we were at practice and wouldn't expect us back for another couple of hours, it was getting to be dusk and would be really dark in about half an hour.

We suddenly started calling out for Mikey again, louder, sounding slightly panicky, I have to admit, and my fearless brother, who had never been afraid of anything in his life and who always treated me like a useless girl, suddenly grabbed my arm.

'What're we goin' to do, Jen?' he said.

I realised then that I was going to be the one to have to come up with something. Simon looked as though he was about to cry.

'Shh,' I said. 'Be quiet, let's just listen for a bit.' I sat down on a tree stump and hoped there were no ants crawling around.

So we sat. I tried to see the sky but the trees were so thick it was hard to see much.

Then, 'What's that?' Gazza pointed towards the way we had just come. 'See, there's a light and it's moving.'

Excited, we looked at a light which seemed to be moving among the trees, but suddenly it stopped, then rose quickly, moving so fast it was hard to believe such a thing was possible, and we gazed in disbelief as it disappeared for a moment and then reappeared high up in a tree, and then was quite still. It flickered for a moment then went out and it was dark again.

'What was that?' Simon whispered.

'Dunno,' I said and looked at Gazza, who seemed to be in a trance, staring up into the tree. I gave him a push. 'Come on,' I said as I heaved myself up and brushed off my pants. 'Let's go back to the other path. It came from that direction.'

'What'ya doin', Jen?' Gazza was tugging at my arm. 'We don't know what that thing is. What kind of creature can be all lit up like that and then fly up into the trees? We don't know what we're dealing with here. We don't have any protection.' He was picking up a long branch from the ground and pulling bits off it to make a stick.

A lot of use that'd be, I thought.

'Perhaps it's a tree monster.' Simon was hugging himself, eyes wide with fright. 'S'pose it jumps down on us.'

I put my arm around him. 'Come on, Simon, there's no tree monsters, there's gotta be a rational explanation. It'll be OK, you'll see. Just stay close to me.' I tried to sound more confident than I felt.

This time, they followed me with Bazza in the rear as I headed back to where I hoped the original path was. It wasn't too far and I recognised a big tree stump right on the corner. So we started back the way we had come, towards the main road. I was trying to follow the original path we had cleared the way through, then I stopped suddenly and Simon, who was close behind, bumped into me. I had seen something glistening on the ground and bent over to have a better look, then picked up a mobile phone with a picture of a tiger on the cover, which had opened itself up.

'What is it?' Gazza reached out to take it from my hand.

'It's Mikey's phone,' I said, in slight disbelief, I have to admit, as I handed it to him. 'That means he has to be around here somewhere.'

'Mikey,' we all called again then, loudly, hopefully, looking around, looking up.

'Ssh!' I told them. 'I think I heard something.'

So we listened and then I heard it again. The distant sound of some-one calling,

'Hello, hello,' from up ahead.

We started running then as well as we could, pushing through the bush, bumping into one another. and panting until…

'Thank goodness,' I puffed. I could see the bulky outline of our car through the thinning trees and, glory be, someone sitting on the bonnet waving.

'Mikey, are you all right?' I gasped as the others behind me came to a halt. I wanted to give him a hug and weep with relief but that wouldn't do in front of Gazza, who was starting to berate him.

'Where did you go? Didn't you hear us calling you? We've been looking for you.'

Mikey jumped down from the bonnet and faced Gazza. He looked upset, white and clearly scared. 'I didn't know where you were. I thought you were all lost. I had to go for a pee and called out to you to wait for me but you didn't, and then I tried to catch up but you'd dis-appeared. So then I got my phone to call to find out where you were but it was dead and then I put the torch on so I could see and that's when it grabbed it and ran off and my mum's gonna kill me for losing it.'

Gazza had calmed down now that he had seen how upset Mikey was. He handed him his phone. 'There you go, Mikey,' he said and managed a small laugh. 'Now you won't get killed at least.'

Mikey grabbed his phone and clutched it to his chest. He inspected it closely. 'Hey, the signal's back,' he said. 'Where did you find it?' Relief was written all over his face.

'Back there on the path,' Gazza told him. 'Whoever grabbed it must have dropped it.' He sounded a little puzzled. 'Who could have taken it from you? He turned to me. 'We saw no one else, did we? Not a soul.' He looked again at Mikey. 'What did he look like?'

Mikey wiped his eyes which had started to water over and tried to think. 'I didn't really see it,' he said.

'It?' I said. 'You mean it wasn't a person?'

'I don't know. I just saw this hand. It came from behind. I didn't hear it or see it. It was just so quick. Just a big hairy hand with a lot of fingers and black fingernails.' He pondered. 'It must have been a monkey, mustn't it?'

'It must have taken it up in the tree when we saw the light moving,' Simon offered.

'Mikey,' I said gently, 'this is Australia. We don't have bush monkeys. It couldn't have been a monkey unless it had escaped from a zoo or something.'

There was silence then as we all pondered the unexplainable. I wondered how it had managed to switch the torch off.

Then Gazza was back to reality. 'Look, we better get going.' He turned to me. 'Can you phone Jack and tell him we're a bit late but we're on our way.'

Things were back to normal. Gazza telling me what to do and me doing it.

Well, almost normal. What was not normal was my brother saying, like an afterthought, 'Thanks. Jen.'

Arthur Biggins

Arthur Biggins didn't notice that he was getting old. He had lost count of time since his wife Pammy had died. They had never been blessed with children, so there was no one to remind him when another birthday came around.

Arthur never bothered to look in the mirror. There was only one anyway, and that was a small one over the bathroom sink. There was a big one behind the dressing table in the main bedroom, but when Pammy had passed. Arthur had closed the bedroom door and never went in there again. He slept in the single bed in the other room.

His beard was long and sometimes he found a pair of scissors and chopped a bit off the bottom and the bit overhanging his mouth so that he could eat without food getting caught in his whiskers. He did notice one day. though, with some surprise. that he wasn't as tall as he used to be. He went to reach up to the shelf at the top of the wardrobe, where he kept a suitcase and a box of old stuff which he had forgotten about, and had to fetch the small stool from the kitchen to stand on.

He dragged the box down and opened it up. Old photographs mostly. Pammy must have put them away, he thought. He tipped them all out and rifled through, looking closely at the pictures, recognising no one and none of the places where they had been taken. So returning everything to the box, he took it out and dumped the lot into the recycling bin. Then he went back inside and heaved the suitcase down and dropped it onto the floor.

Arthur had on old friend, Wally Baxter. They caught up every couple of weeks and went to the pub for lunch and a beer or two. Wally had a son, grown-up now with a family who often spent weekends at their shack down on the coast; sometimes Wally went along too,

'You should come along,' Wally told Arthur. 'They're going away for a coupla weeks and I'm going to stay at the shack for a bit while they're away. How about coming with me next weekend? I'll drive. I've still got my licence, you know.' He had noted Arthur's incredulous look. 'I've had the old Volvo serviced and it's good to go. Take two or three hours to get there. What d'you reckon then? Are you game, mate? Might cheer you up a bit.'

So, after much deliberating, Arthur had agreed.

Early on Saturday morning, he went into the bathroom and, after a good shower ,went to have a look in the bathroom mirror. It was all steamy and he cleaned it off with the face flannel.

When did my beard go white, he wondered. It used to be a gingery colour. Must be the glass, he thought, and fingered a crack that he couldn't remember ever seeing there before. He felt the top of his head. His hair seemed thinner, sparse. Funny that, he thought. I never noticed.

He finished packing the old suitcase, not sure what he was supposed to take. Arthur hadn't shopped for clothes for years. Pammy had seen to all that. He had an old blue tracksuit which went into the washing machine occasionally, a few pairs of threadbare jocks and socks. He had his sneakers, well worn but still comfortable, a new pair of pyjamas which were still in the plastic bag and never been worn. He had always worn jocks and a T-shirt to bed but he thought that if he was going away, perhaps he should take the pyjamas, There were a few T-shirts he could pack and most of last fortnight's pension money was stuffed into his wallet. No credit cards. Arthur didn't believe in them.

By nine o'clock, Arthur was ready and waiting by the front gate. He was wearing his one good pair of jeans that were kept for special occasions and a blue T-shirt which had still been in its original bag.

When Wally pulled up alongside the kerb right on time, Arthur stared for a moment. Wally wasn't wearing his cap today. He'd never seen him without his cap. When did Wally go bald? he asked himself.

He said nothing, though, as he threw his suitcase into the back and then settled himself into the passenger seat.

'How ya going, mate?' Wally gave him a grin. 'Everything OK?'

'Good mate, good.' Arthur was feeling an unaccustomed little bit of excitement as they set off.

Wally drove carefully, his foot continually touching the brake. Arthur sat back, trying to relax. He hadn't been driving for years. Shops were only a short walk from home, as was the bus stop if he needed to go to town. He had no desire to go travelling, enjoyed his garden and looked after himself as best as he could; he even enjoyed cooking. Since Pammy had gone, he hadn't had the heart to go travelling on his own.

Wally put the radio on and Arthur sat back and looked at the passing countryside, which he thought seemed a bit blurry in the distance. Perhaps, he thought, I should get my eyes tested.

He cupped a hand to his ear as he realised Wally was talking. 'What?' he asked.

'I said, we could stop for lunch at Port Wakefield,' Wally shouted.

'Okay, sure.' Arthur nodded. He turned the radio down. He didn't recognise any of the music that was playing. He wished they would play some of the old songs which had real singalong tunes and words he could understand.

It was a good day for a drive. About twenty-four degrees and the beginning of summer promising warmer days ahead.

They arrived at Port Wakefield about half an hour later.

Arthur staggered a bit getting out of the car. His muscles had stiffened up after so much sitting and he noticed Wally was having the same problem. He made a face. 'Not getting any younger,' he remarked.

They found a pub and lingered a bit over the pie and a beer until Wally said, 'Better get going then, if we want to get there before teatime.' His daughter-in-law had left food in the fridge, so they didn't have to worry about shopping for a day or so,

They reached the shack a couple of hours later without incident, thanks to Wally's careful driving. They could smell the salty air, and for a moment, Arthur was taken back to his childhood and the excitement he felt when going on summer holidays with his sister. He gazed at the beach and the water, calm and inviting. He could remember the time when he would have thrown off his clothes, revelling in the feel of sand between his toes, laughing and yelling with joy as he made his first plunge into the cool water.

'Whatcha reckon, then?' Wally was saying after they had let themselves into the small wooden shack.

It was on a grassy clearing with steps leading down to the beach. There was a rail to hang on to as well, Arthur saw with relief.

'It's great, mate,' he said,

The power was on and a small fridge humming away. They found some beers Wally's son had left for them and a couple of fold-up chairs which they took outside onto the little veranda. The sun was getting low in the sky off to the west and it looked as though there might be a good sunset.

They lifted their bottles.

'Cheers, mate.'

They both said it at the same time, then Wally nudged Arthur and pointed towards the beach, where two women in colourful bathers were walking along the sand.

Arthur shaded his eyes and watched for a moment or two. Then he thought that perhaps tomorrow he would trim his beard.

Smiley Face

One

The house Emily had rented for a couple of weeks lived up to its name. and she was fairly happy with it. Beach Side Cottage, it said. All conveniences and fully furnished. So she had booked it, sight unseen, and so far it had lived up to expectations. It was overlooking the beach and the quaint old-fashioned furniture was comfortable. The kitchen was fully equipped and the big double bed looked inviting, although she hadn't had a chance to try it out yet.

Emily and Simon had found the key under the pot plant as instructed, let themselves in, unpacked and had a picnic lunch with food they had brought with them. Then they had explored the beach and Simon had helped her settle in. So it wasn't until later on that afternoon that Emily realised the lights didn't work.

Simon had looked up to the ceiling. 'No light globes,' he said.

So they checked the rest of the house. There was one bedside lamp with no globe and none in any of the other rooms. They searched all the cupboards; there weren't many of those and came up with nothing.

'What about candles?' said Emily. 'Surely there are some candles.'

But no, there was no sign of any candles either.

Simon had been checking out the car, which had been playing up a bit. He had driven his mother to the small seaside town and it had been a long drive. There had been a little clunking noise which he had been concerned about.

'While you're fixing the car, I'll walk up to the village,' Emily said. 'We came through it on the way and it's not that far. I need the exercise. I'll see if I can find a shop that sells light globes and I'll check out the local pub as well,' she added, 'see what their meals look like.'

'Take your phone,' he told her. 'Just in case you get lost.' He grinned. His mother had a habit of getting lost.

So she had started walking up the hill to the village shops, about ten minutes, she reckoned. It was a straight road and no turnoffs, so no way she could get lost, and that was a plus.

The shopping centre was a typical village main street, all the little shops selling their speciality. She couldn't see a supermarket, so started at the first shop on the left-hand side of the street. It was closed; a real estate agent's office with pictures of houses and land for sale on the windows. There was also a sign on the door which read 'Closed until further notice due to bereavement' plus alongside it someone had drawn a picture of a sad face with one curl sticking up on the top of its head.

Emily moved along to the next shop, a hairdressers, and stopped, frowning as she read another sign. This one said, 'Closed until further notice' and another emoji with two curls on the top, squeezed into the corner of the sign. That's a bit strange, thought Emily, as she moved on to the next shop.

She looked at the big sign over the doorway. 'ALBERT'S HARDWARE STORE', it said. Great, Emily thought, I hope this one's open. It's sure to have light globes. Then she stopped short staring unbelievingly at yet another notice, sticky taped to the door. 'GONE FISHING', it said, written in a childish hand with odd-shaped letters. This time there was a happy smiley face drawn next to the message. Rather strange-looking with three big curls sticking up from the top of his head. Emily hoped the writer of the notice was having a good day, because she certainly wasn't.

She looked at her watch. Only four o'clock; it was a bit early to shut up shop, she thought, and carried on along the street. The next shop was open, a butchers. Well, they certainly won't sell light globes, she decided, and carried on. This was turning out to be more difficult than she had thought but, always optimistic, Emily stopped at the next shop, which was also open and hooray, she said to herself, a general store. They would sell everything, wouldn't they?

The old-fashioned bell jangled as she opened the door and she was facing a counter, behind which an elderly lady was beaming brightly at her over spectacles perched on the end of her nose.

'Good afternoon, madam. Can I help you?' she asked.

'I hope so.' Emily smiled back. 'Do you have any light globes?'

The elderly lady, whose name was Annie Spriggs according to the big name tag attached to a ribbon dangling around her neck, suddenly looked sorrowful and a little suspiciously at Emily as she shook her head. 'Oh, I'm so sorry,' she said. 'I'm all out at the moment. Somebody came and bought every last one, A whole box full.' She wrinkled her forehead up in a frown. 'Very strange, I thought. Why would anyone want a dozen light globes?' She stared at Emily. 'Why are you buying light globes as well? What is going on? Anyway, I'm sorry, madam, I can't help you.'

'It's Emily,' Emily said automatically. She certainly was not a madam. 'Well, what about candles then?' Surely there would be candles.

'Did you try Alberts Hardware?' Annie asked her, businesslike now. 'He would have globes and candles, I would have thought. He's just back along the road,' she added helpfully.

Emily nodded. 'Yes, I went there first, but he's shut.'

'Shut? He's never shut.' Annie looked slightly astounded. 'Are you sure? Did you try the door? Sometimes he's inclined to nod off in that old chair behind the counter.'

'Yes,' Emily nodded. 'It was definitely locked, plus there was a sign on the door which said, "Gone fishing", and,' she added, 'there was a picture of a smiley face as well. Quite funny, really, with three curls on its head.'

Annie stood stock still and stopped fiddling with her name tag. She looked shocked. 'Smiley face? Three curls? Gone fishing?' she said un-believingly, 'Old Albert's never gone fishing in his life.' She took her glasses off and gazed at Emily with eyes wide open and apprehensive. Are you sure Mad– er, Emily? Are you sure it was Albert's Hardware shop?'

Emily nodded. 'I'm sure.' she said, then sensed something was amiss as Annie suddenly looked at her watch, came around the counter, grabbed a packet of candles from a shelf on the way and thrust them at her.

'Here,' she said. 'Don't worry about that just now.' She indicated Emily's purse, which she had started to open to find some money. 'You can pay me later.' She pushed Emily towards the door. 'Get back home as quickly as you can. You are down at the beach house, aren't you?'

Feeling puzzled and not a little spooked, Emily stared at the elderly lady, who was now clearly looking panicky for some reason. 'How did you know where I'm staying?' she asked.

'Never you mind about that. Now just you hurry home and be sure to close your windows.' With that, she gave Emily a final little push out onto the pavement.

Emily staggered a bit before righting herself and then saw the door slam and heard a bolt being drawn. She peered through the window, puzzled, and just before all the lights were switched off, saw Annie grab the phone on the counter and start talking animatedly to someone, shaking her head and looking so worried, Emily wondered if she should stay around in case there was anything she could do to help. Then shrugged. Whatever was going on was really none of her business. She started walking back down the road towards the beach, looking around and behind her. The street, which had been bustling with shoppers and people stopping to chat, had suddenly gone very quiet. and Emily realised that all the shops were closing. Shutters were being slammed down, people were hurrying to cars parked on the street and driven off. Not understanding what was happening, she started feeling a little bit scared, which was not in Emily's nature. She was a naturally observant person and whenever something unusual happened, it piqued her curiosity.

She would get to the bottom of it.

Two

'Are you sure you're going to be all right?' Simon looked concerned. He wanted to get going before dark.

Emily nodded. 'I'll be fine. It's just lovely here. Nice and quiet. I'll be able to get some writing done.' She hadn't told Simon about the strange happenings in the village, just that the shops had closed early. She knew he would probably worry, and anyway, she thought, it was most likely nothing except her rather active imagination.

'Just get going.' She gave him a hug. 'I'll see you next week.'

'OK.' Simon opened the car door. 'Be sure to ring me if there are any problems. You'll be right with the candles for now, then you can get some globes tomorrow. Just get there early. Sometimes these villagers make their own rules and close up when they feel like it.'

'I'll be fine.' Emily waved goodbye as he left and turned back to the house.

Thunderous-looking clouds were rolling in and it was getting dark. She hoped Simon would make it back safely before the storm hit, then went to bed early with her writing pad and pen and two candles stuck to saucers on the bedside table. She listened to the thunder as it rolled around the sky with occasional lightning brightening the bedroom. Emily quite liked storms.

The bed was as comfortable as it looked. She tried not to think about missing light globes and the strange behaviour of Annie Spriggs, and instead tried to concentrate on the article she had to write for her column in the local monthly *Tribune*.

Her large lined pad was still beside her on the bed when she woke next morning and the only thing written on it was 'SMILEY FACE' in large letters right across the top. Must have been tired, she thought. I don't remember writing that.

After a walk along the beach that morning, breakfast, coffee and setting up her laptop, Emily started out again for her trek to the village shops, making sure she had her phone in her bag. She had a shopping list this time, needing some items from the general store as well as paying for the candles.

Everything seemed to be normal. Shops were open but there were very few people about and not many cars parked. Emily stopped short as she reached the main street. Down the road, she could see two police cars parked outside Albert's Hardware and policemen conferring on the pavement.

She stopped at the first shop. The sign was still there, so was the sign on the hairdresser's window. Then she reached Albert's Hardware store and came to a halt. The 'Gone Fishing' sign had disappeared. It has been replaced with another one: 'CLOSED'. Just that, 'CLOSED'.

One of the policemen approached. 'Just move along please,' he said.

'What's going on?' Emily didn't move.

'Are you a member of Albert Hardcastle's family?' he asked

'No, I'm visiting,' she replied.

'In that case, move along.' He eyed the few people who were gathering around. 'Clear the area,' he shouted now. 'Come on now, move away, there's nothing for you to see here.'

'What's happened to Albert?' It was the butcher from next door looking anxious.

The policeman didn't answer; he was getting agitated. Again he shouted, 'Go home, all of you.'

There was muttering then, and reluctantly the small crowd dispersed.

The butcher went back into his shop and Emily slowly walked to the general store, to see if it was open. The door was slightly ajar, so she went inside.

Annie was in her place behind the counter. But there was no welcoming smile today. She looked tired, her eyes were red and she was clutching a handkerchief.

'I want to thank you for the candles and to pay for them,' Emily started. She wasn't sure what to say – this lady was obviously shaken – but then her naturally kind instinct kicked in. 'Is there anything I can do for you, Annie? You look upset. Has something happened to Albert? There are police cars outside.'

Annie didn't say anything for a long moment, then she blew her nose hard into her handkerchief, wiped her eyes, stood up straight and looked Emily in the eye. 'Albert's dead!' she said.

Feeling shocked, Emily regarded Annie with sympathy and searched for words of condolence. 'I'm so sorry,' she said. 'I guess you must have known him for a long time. What happened, Annie? Was he ill?'

'No, he was fine yesterday, and then I found him this morning,' Annie told her. 'He was just sitting in his armchair and I thought he was asleep, but then when he didn't move when I touched him, I realised he wasn't breathing, so I called the ambulance.' Annie wiped her eyes and carried on. 'His sister Betty rang me this morning and asked me to go and check that he was OK because he didn't come home last night – he lives with his sister, you see, and I have a key for emergencies – but she didn't worry because sometimes he sleeps in the shop. He worried about break-ins, although I don't know why – there hasn't been a break-in in this area for years – but I knew something was wrong when you told me about the sign on the window, I should have checked then but I was too freaked out and hoped it was a coincidence.' Annie stopped talking to get a breath and wiped her eyes.

Emily was confused. 'You've lost me, Annie. Why what was a coincidence?'

'Because of the smiley face.'

'The smiley face?'

'Yes, the smiley face with three curls.'

'Oh?'

Annie looked at Emily for a long moment; she seemed to be making up her mind about something. She saw a pair of calm blue eyes under a grey fringe and a reassuring friendly smile and made a decision. 'OK then, I'll try to explain,' she said, 'but you'll probably think I'm being silly.'

'I promise I won't.' Emily smiled and nodded encouragingly.

'You saw that the real estate agents was closed?' Annie started and continued, 'Well, Barry, that was his name, apparently fell and hit his head on the corner of his desk. He was alone at the time and was found by a customer, but he died as a result of his injuries, they said. But no one knows why he fell. Of course,' Annie added, 'it was well known that he always had a bottle under his desk and who knows, he could have um…overindulged. Be that as it may, the other thing is, nobody knows who put the sad face on the sign.' Annie stopped talking and blew her nose again then added, 'The first time I saw it, I didn't think much about it.'

'So?' Emily was getting curious now. 'OK, that's a bit odd, I must admit, but nothing to worry about, I shouldn't think,' she said, 'but what happened to the hairdresser then?'

'Well, that's another strange thing, you see,' Annie continued. 'Nancy was quite aged and should have retired by now but she was a good hairdresser and still had all her customers, but the wiring in that hairdressers needed redoing, it was antiquated, and Nancy never wanted to spend the money. Sometimes the lights blew out. They think she must have dropped a hair dryer into the basin by accident and been electrocuted which gave her a heart attack. But there were no customers in there at the time, so why was she using the hair dryer? Unless she decided to wash her own hair. Plus, the thing is, there was another sad face only this one had two curls on the top. I saw it myself after I saw the one at the real estate agent's place and that had only one curl on the top.'

Annie stopped for breath again and looked at Emily, who thought she could see where this was headed.

'Yes, I see now,' she said slowly, 'so when I mentioned that the smiley face on Albert's window had three curls, I understand how that would have seemed a bit strange.' Emily looked thoughtful. 'Three curls, three deaths. Very creepy. I expect your imagination ran away with you and you were wondering where the next smiley face with four curls would appear?'

She half tried to make a joke of it, but Annie wasn't smiling. She nodded, looking uncertain. 'Seems stupid, doesn't it!' she gave a rueful smile.

'What did Albert die of?' Emily asked, intrigued now, but Annie shook her head.

'They don't know. They think his heart just stopped, I suppose that can happen – he used to smoke a lot – but who knows, the ambulance man said they might have to do an autopsy.' She stopped talking and thought for a moment 'How could he lock the door if he was already dead?' Annie said.

Emily was thinking hard. 'Perhaps he was feeling ill and locked the door and then sat down.'

Annie nodded again. 'I s'pose that could happen, but then,' she added, 'why would someone put that sign up?'

'I don't know,' Emily admitted. 'Maybe someone did it for a joke when they found the door locked. Maybe children, or the same ones who did the others.' She pulled out her shopping list. 'Annie, are you opening the shop for business today? I have a few things I need if you're up to it. I really think you should go home and rest, though. Is there anyone else who can help you?

'Yes, I could ask my friend Mabel. She often lends a hand when I have to go to the doctor's or somewhere. In fact, I rang her yesterday after you told me about the third smiley face. I told her all about it. She said I was imagining things,' Annie said. Then she straightened up, put her glasses back on and, almost back to her own cheerful self, smiled at Emily. 'Thank you for listening to a silly old woman,' she said, 'and, by the way, a new batch of light globes will be in this morning. They're those newfangled ones which are supposed to save the electricity. That's probably why they all sold so quick – everybody's replacing the old ones.'

Well, that solved one mystery, thought Emily. 'I don't think you're silly at all,' she said. 'In fact, I think it's all very curious to say the least.' Emily had to admit there were a few thing which didn't add up. But she was pleased to hear that she would be able to get some light globes. There was one thing that she wanted to know, however. 'Why did you tell me to hurry home yesterday and why did everyone suddenly close up shop?'

'Well, that was because of the storm. We get fierce storms here.

Word got around and everyone agreed to pack up early. The weather bureau let me know yesterday just before you came into the shop.'

And that's solved another mystery, Emily decided as she collected her shopping. The light globes were delivered just as she was about to leave, so that was a relief, but a niggling question was still winding its way through her brain.

Three

Emily decided to check something out and wasn't game to approach the grumpy policeman, who was still ordering people around, so after a quick look along the street, she made her way to the end of the block of shops and went around the back to a laneway, where she had guessed there would be some rubbish bins.

There they were, all in line ready for collection. The 'Gone Fishing' sign must have been put somewhere, she decided, so this was worth a try.

'HARDWARE SHOP' was written in big letters on one of the bins and Emily lifted the lid feeling guilty, hoping no one would spot her looking in a bin like a bag lady. She shifted some boxes out of the way and 'Bingo,' she muttered as she picked up a crumpled piece of paper. She straightened it out. 'GONE FISHING' was a bit damp in one corner but still quite readable. Quickly she put it into her shopping bag, had another look around, then returned to the front of the shops.

She went back along to the hairdressers and took a closer look at the sign. Bringing out the other one from her bag, she compared the writing, The writing was different and done with a biro. But the sad face was not. It was done with, she guessed, a blue texta, the same as Albert's. She hurried along now to the real estate office. This sign was typed but the face was drawn with a similar blue texta.

Across the street, a small café was open with tables and chairs out the front under umbrellas, so Emily crossed the road and went inside, ordered a coffee and piece of cheesecake, then settled herself on one of the outside chairs. She needed to have a bit of a think.

Her phone buzzed. It was Simon sending a text. He was just checking everything was OK and reminding her to keep in touch. Emily sent a message back telling him that she now had light globes and everything was fine. As she was about to send, she pressed the wrong button and brought up all the emojis, and with a gasp realised that the faces on the shop signs were similar to the ones on her phone.

She pressed send before bringing up the emojis again and compared them with the picture on Albert's sign. There was no doubt that this was a copy, plus the smiley face, and the writing as well, was done with a similar blue texta.

Emily closed her eyes, trying to remember the faces on the real estate agent's and hairdressers. Were they the same? She thought not.

She was still trying to visualise them when a worried sounding girl's voice said, 'Are you OK, madam?'

Emily opened her eyes to see her coffee being placed before her on the table. 'Oh, sorry,' she smiled. 'I'm fine, just thinking,'

The young woman smiled back. 'Just so's you're OK then. Enjoy your coffee.'

She had only just taken one sip when an elderly gentleman with beautiful whiskers emerged from inside the café and sat himself down in the other chair at Emily's table.

He held out his hand. 'Good morning, Mrs Hobson,' he smiled. 'Welcome to my coffee shop. I hope you find it to your taste.'

He spoke with an accent. Greek, she thought.

'It's Emily,' she said as she shook, 'and yes, the coffee is very good, thank you.' She was thinking quickly. 'How long have you been here, Mr...?'

'George Papadopulous,' he beamed. 'Ten years now,' he said. 'Such a beautiful place, good people all around. Are you enjoying your stay at the beach house?'

Emily was bemused at this remark. How come everyone knows my name and where I live, she pondered.

'Yes, thanks,' she smiled at him.

'I hear you're a writer,' he said then.

'How did you know…? Emily started.

'Ah,' he broke in, 'that was Barry, the real estate agent. He owned that house. He told everyone you were coming.' George stopped talking and looked sad. 'Such a pity,' he said. 'So sad, passing away like that.' He shook his head. 'His funeral was last week. Everybody went. Then there was Nancy's just a few days later!'

'And now,' said Emily, 'There's poor Albert. A sad time for everyone I should think. Everybody in this village seems to know everyone else – like a big family.' She smiled a little sadly. 'It's good really when something awful like this happens, everyone supports everyone else, don't they?'

George reached over and patted her hand. 'I see you understand,' he said. 'I think you'll fit right in here, I can see that.' He rose from the table. 'I must go. I expect I'll see you again, Mrs Hobson.'

'It's Emily,' she told him again.

He waved his hand as he left. 'Oh, OK then,' he said. 'See you later, Emily.'

She finished her coffee, which was indeed good, and polished off the cheesecake. Then, gathering up her shopping, Emily walked slowly home. She had some thinking to do and she had to get started on her column for the *Tribune* – the deadline was in two days.

Emily had been writing her monthly piece for the *Tribune* for around five years now; an unlikely journalist, she had an unobtrusive gentle manner and the ability to blend in with the background. No one paid her much attention, which was just the way she liked it. She observed people and was a splendid judge of character, managing to obtain information without intruding into people's lives. Her columns always had a rural touch and, although they were basically founded on truth, it must be admitted there was sometimes a little fiction inserted if, in Emily's opinion, the story needed spicing up a bit!

She was feeling mildly excited today. Her story this time would of course be set around the curious events in this seaside village occurring over the past couple of days. The interesting people she had met, the great little community and beautiful surroundings. She had got the bulk of it done and was quite pleased. But there was a niggle she couldn't ignore. Who had drawn the faces? Maybe it wasn't important enough to worry about, thought Emily, but there again, her natural curiosity was getting the better of her. She needed to know.

She saved everything she had written so far. Made a cup of coffee and sat down for a good think.

It was just as she was taking a sip that she was reminded of the little café and George. She closed her eyes. There was something she knew she knew but couldn't remember. Then suddenly it came. One of the tables in the corner had large pieces of paper and coloured pencils in a jam jar, put there no doubt to keep children occupied; a good idea taken up in many cafés these days.

Of course, she thought. Children. It had to be. Obvious! Admitted, she had seen no children yesterday, but they would have been at school, wouldn't they.

So tomorrow, she thought, perhaps just to satisfy herself, she would go back to the village and ask George who he thought the culprit or culprits might be, then she would be able to finish her story and send it off in good time. Or, she thought, she could finish the story today with a mention of childish pranks. The sign on Albert's door would no doubt have been done by someone who found the door locked and did it as a joke. The other two would just have been sad signs for sad occasions.

So, making a decision, Emily sat down at her laptop again and wrote another paragraph with a humorous touch about childish pranks, coffee shops, sad faces and smiley faces. She did another brief edit and then with a happy satisfied smile sent it off to her editor.

For the next few days, Emily went on a few bus trips exploring the local area, sat by the beach, took walks and did a lot of reading, so it wasn't until the following Friday that she went back up to the shops.

She called in to see Annie. who told her that Albert had definitely died of a heart attack and that the funeral would be next week. She didn't mention smiley faces, so Emily didn't either, in spite of a niggle of curiosity which wouldn't go away.

She went to see George at his coffee shop, who gave her a big welcome and insisted on giving her a coffee on the house, so, after a friendly chat, Emily asked him about the drawing paper and pencils.

'Ah,' he said, 'that's there for the tourists. It keeps their kids occupied, then they stay longer and maybe buy more coffee and cake.' George laughed. 'Keeps my wife happy too, as she makes the cakes.'

'What about local children? Do they come in and do it too? Draw pictures?' Emily wanted to know.

'No,' he said. 'Not so much, maybe on school holidays when they've got nothing else to do. That will start next Monday and then we'll all be busy for a couple of weeks.'

George stood up, collecting her now empty coffee cup. 'So when are you leaving us, Emily?' he asked her.

'On Sunday,' Emily told him. 'My son will be picking me up. I would have liked to stay longer, this is such a lovely place. I'll call in again before I go.'

She bade him goodbye then and wandered along the shopping strip picking up a few souvenirs along the way.

She found a SMILEY FACE fridge magnet and added it to her shopping bag.

Four

On Sunday morning, Emily slept in for a little while before getting up. She tidied the house and packed, wanting to be ready when Simon arrived, so it wasn't until later on in the morning that she decided to have last look around outside to make sure there was nothing left behind.

She stepped out onto the little porch then, as she turned to close the door, she stopped, totally shocked, at the sight of the attached notice.

A smiley face had been drawn onto a large sheet of paper. This was a happy one done in the same blue texta as the others but there were red hearts where the eyes would have been. There were also four curls on the top and alongside was the word 'GOODBYE', written with a wobbly hand, no doubt by the same person who wrote Albert's sign.

Emily was still staring at it when Simon pulled up.

He waved as Emily went to greet him. 'Are you okay, Mum?' He looked concerned. 'You look like you've seen a ghost!'

'I'm fine. It's just that I found this.' Emily showed him. 'It's like the others.'

'What others? What's this all about?'

So she told him. All about the other smiley faces. Simon of course, being a very logical practical person, reinforced what she had already decided. He said it was the work of a prankster who in this case must be a friend who was going to miss her. That he thought it was cool and nothing to worry about and wasn't it time that they got going, They could stop for lunch on the way home.

So Emily put it out of her head, although she carefully folded the sign and stowed it into her bag. They stopped briefly at the village shops, where she popped in to say goodbye to Annie, who gave her a hug and told her to keep in touch, and George, who introduced himself to Simon and told him he was lucky to have such a lovely mother. She waved goodbye to a couple of people as they passed by, then they were on their way home.

Back at the coffee house, a twelve-year-old boy was sitting at the children's table looking at a phone. Benny went to a special school which always had longer school holidays than the regular schools. He was learning to write and liked to draw. Everyone knew and loved George's grandson, who came to stay with his grandparents on school holidays. He felt at home in the village, knew everyone and roamed around greeting all his friends with a big smile. They all kept an eye on him. Benny understood more than people realised but rarely communicated with anybody, so it was hard to know sometimes what he was thinking.

'Are you looking at the pictures on my phone again, Benny?' George bent over him and tousled his curly black hair.

Benny looked up at him and smiled. His was a happy face.

Trespassers

'TRESPASSERS WILL BE PERSECUTED' said the sign, painted in large black letters. It was wired to the gate and looked quite new.

'Well, I'll be…' remarked old Tom. 'Haven't noticed that before.' He turned to his mate. 'What d'you reckon, Alf? You seen that there sign before?'

Alf scratched his nearly bald pate. 'Nup, never seen that before,' he said. 'Who d'you reckon put that up there then?'

Old Tom went over and rattled the gate. 'Well, it's not locked. Maybe we could take a chance and go through anyway.'

Alf shook his head. 'Better not risk it. Don't want to get persecuted, do we.'

'Well, what happens when you get persecuted then?'

'Dunno, take you off to the cop shop most likely and put you in a cell.'

'Nah, they wouldn't do that. I've known Shorty nearly all me life. He's a good copper. He'd probably just give us a warning or something.'

'Well, what are we going to do?' Alf was getting agitated. 'We always take a short cut over this paddock to get to the high street, If we have to walk all the way round, my legs'll give out, and 'sides, the guys will wonder where we are and might start without us.'

The weekly game of cards had become routine for the old mates every Saturday afternoon at Arthur's place. For some, it was the highlight of the week. Alf and Old Tom never missed. It was only a ten-minute slow walk as a rule from their street, but if they had to walk all rround the paddock, it would be more like a half hour.

Alf shook the gate. 'What's in there that's so special anyway? What are they trying to hide?' He peered over the gate, shading his eyes. 'Can't see much. Just some mangy-looking cows having a munch.' He chuckled. 'Not that there's much to munch on. Since the big long dry we've been having, all the grass has disappeared. Poor buggers!'

Old Tom looked resigned. 'Well, I guess we'd better start walking. I'm not going to risk getting a police record at my age. Come on, mate, it won't be that bad. We can take it easy and if we're late, then we're late.'

'Well, how're we getting back home? I can't see us walking all the way round again.' Alf was getting more agitated. 'I reckon we might as well go back home again now.'

Old Tom wasn't having any of that. 'Don't worry, mate. You know Billy T always has his son drop him off. Well, we can always ask him to give us a lift home. He's a good bloke. He wont mind. Come on now, let's get going.'

So they got going. They were halfway round the paddock, walking along the road that ran alongside it, when Alf suddenly stopped.

He grabbed Old Tom's arm. 'Shh,' he whispered, 'get down, don't let him see you!'

'Who?'

'Him, over there, see? A bloke with a gun, a big gun looks like.'

They both crouched down behind a sparse hedge growing alongside the road and peered through.

'What's he doing? said Alf. 'Can you see?'

Old Tom was shading his eyes. 'He's probably looking for rabbits or something. Come on, mate, let's get going. He's not going to worry about us.'

'He's up to no good.' Alf wasn't about to budge. 'See, he's got a spade. I couldn't see it before. It must've been behind that bush. Now he's digging a hole. See, I told you that fella's up to no good. What's he digging a hole for? What's he burying then?'

The man had taken a red shirt off and had thrown it on the ground. He was wearing a singlet which only partially covered the tattoos across his arms and back and his long hair was falling over his face as he frantically dug, glancing around every few moments.

'See. I told you, he's up to no good,' whispered Alf.

Old Tom was interested now. 'I think you're right,' he said, 'but my back's killing me. I have to sit down for a bit,' and he gingerly lowered himself to the ground.

'Good idea.' Alf followed suit.

The old mates watched the man, curious, a little tremor of excitement stirring them both, the game of cards temporarily forgotten.

Suddenly Alf grabbed Old Tom's arm again. 'Look. Over there, see that cow?'

'Yes, what about it?'

'I think it's a bull!'

Then they watched, transfixed, as the bull, which had spotted the bloke in his paddock, decided to investigate. His gentle saunter turned into a charge. The man digging the hole looked up and saw the bull coming straight for him. He gave a yell, dropped the spade, picked up the rifle and aimed it at the charging bull. He had time to fire one shot but in his hurry missed. The bull kept charging and the man just turned and ran for his life, heading towards the entrance which had the NO TRESPASSERS sign up. Neither of the old mates could speak for a moment.

'I never knew there was a bull in there with that lot, did you?' then asked Old Tom.

Alf shook his head. 'All the years I've been across that paddock and I've never seen a bull.'

'Well, that fella sure wasn't expecting one either,' remarked Old Tom. He looked across the paddock. 'Seems like he's gone.' He was trying to struggle to his feet. 'I guess we'd better get up. Give us a hand, mate.' So they helped each other up then dusted their pants off.

'Well, that sure got rid of him, didn't it?'

'Sure did.' Old Tom was looking at the hedge and pulling dead branches away, revealing a hole with broken chicken wire at the back He pulled at the chicken wire. 'I reckon we can get through here. This fence is all busted. Anyone could get through here.'

They both knew what they were going to do. They looked across the paddock to where the bull was. It was still at the gate but there was no sign of the tattooed man.

'Quick, in case he comes back,' said Alf.

So squeezing through, trying not to snag their clothes on the wire, they made their way over to the where the hole was being dug.

Old Tom whistled, 'Well, I'll be…!

They both stared at an old briefcase which was just visible through a thin layer of soil.

'Quick, let's get it out before he comes back.' Alf was reaching into the hole. 'Come on, give us a hand.'

So between them both, one each side of the hole, they finally managed to drag it out then, wasting no more time, took turns carrying the case back and pushing it through the hole in the fence.

They were both a bit out of breath after all that and Alf gasped, 'Well, what are we going to do with it now then?'

They looked more closely at the briefcase. It was the sort that had a combination lock.

'No way we can open that,' said Old Tom. 'You have to know the combination. I know because my son had one.' He grabbed hold of the handle. 'It's not too heavy. We can take turns carrying it. We're not too far from Arthur's place now, so we can take it there and then decide what to do.'

'We'll have to tell Shorty, won't we?' said Alf, sounding worried. 'And then we're going to have to tell him we went in the paddock which had a NO TRESPASSERS sign up. Do you reckon he'll persecute us?'

Old Tom gave a little smile at that and shook his head. 'No way, not when we give him this. Who knows,' he added, 'we may even get a medal. It could be buried loot!'

When twenty minutes later they finally arrived at Arthur's place, Jimbo, Young Tom (who was only five years younger than Old Tom), Derro and Billy T were looking anxious, then relieved and full of questions. So after some beers were broken into, the two old mates related their story. There may have been a few embellishments, especially when the gun was mentioned, but in the end everyone agreed they should tell the police and they gathered around the kitchen table, unplayed cards scattered about. Arthur's missus brought in some scones and then they all quietened as Arthur called the police station on his landline.

Shorty appeared soon afterwards, looking a little bit excited, which was very unusual. He was about six feet five inches tall, a morose-looking beanpole of a man who took his job as local police sergeant very seriously, but his craggy face broke into a mile as he surveyed the briefcase. 'OK, you two,' he said, casting his eyes upon Old Tom and then Alf. 'You'd better tell me what this is all about then. For starters, where did you find this?' He indicated the briefcase.

So they took it in turns to tell him, leaving nothing out, except about the sign on the gate, but as they didn't actually go through the gate, it didn't seem to matter. But when they described the tattooed man, Shorty started scribbling furiously in his notebook.

'Do you know this bloke then?' Old Tom ventured to ask, but there was no reply.

When the sergeant finally left Arthur's place carrying the briefcase, there wasn't much enthusiasm for resuming any card playing, so they just had another couple of beers and went over the day's happenings a few more times, leaving many unanswered questions, but Shorty had told Old Tom that he would be in touch and they had to settle for that.

Billy T's son gave Old Tom and Alf a lift home, Old Tom to his cottage, where he had stayed after his wife had passed away, and Alf to his sister's place next door.

It wasn't until the following Wednesday that both the old mates were summoned to the police station. They arrived together, a little excited, it must be said, and Shorty sat them down in his office and regarded them with his serious face.

'OK, you two,' he started. 'First of all, you took a big chance. If that fellow had seen you, you would have been shot, no question. Next time you see something strange going on, you call the police station.'

'We didn't have any phone,' said Alf.

'You should always carry phones. Next thing,' Shorty continued, 'there was, of course, money in that briefcase, lots of money. Stolen about a year ago from someone who was about to buy drugs. He was shot and the money disappeared. The man with the tattoos was paid to recover the money from where it had been buried. He said he was just following orders and had no idea what was in the briefcase. That of course is debatable.'

'Did you catch him then?' Old Tom wanted to know.

'Yes, we had him on record, a nasty piece of work. His fingerprints were on the spade and we found his shirt across the paddock, which came in handy for the forensics. We caught him and he came clean. He dobbed in the rest. He said no amount of money was worth getting killed by a bull!'

The policeman stopped talking for a moment and regarded the two old mates. 'Thanks to you two, that's one more unsolved case which is getting sorted out. Plus,' he added, 'a reward has been decided in thanks for your community spirit, even though you acted stupidly by putting yourselves in danger!' He handed over two envelopes. 'There you go.'

Shorty stood up and shook hands with both men, who seemed to have been struck dumb, until Old Tom said, 'Thanks, Shorty.'

Shorty nodded, his serious face on again. 'It's sergeant when I'm on duty,' he said, then held the door for them as they left.

They were out of sight of the police station and sitting in the bar of the local pub before they opened their envelopes,

'Wow!' Old Tom regarded his cheque for $200. 'Well, I'll be…!'

'Whoopee.' Alf jumped up and sat down again with excitement. 'What do you reckon? How good is that!'

Next Saturday arvo, the pair were on their way again to Arthur's place and stopped by the gate leading to the paddock. They had left early, leaving plenty of time for the expected walk. They stopped in amazement.

'Look. The sign's gone!' Alf exclaimed.

'Yeah, how about that?'

'Wonder why it was there in the first place.' Alf was busy opening the gate.

'It was because of the bull.'

'The bull? Why?'

'Well, Arthur told me that he knows the bloke who owns the paddock and he hired the bull to be friendly-like with the cows, plus bulls are expensive and they didn't want to risk it getting out, so he put the sign up to stop nosy parkers who might leave the gate open.' He looked at Alf's face. 'Sorry, mate, I should have told you before.'

'So the bull's gone then?'

'Looks like it, yep.'

'So we're not likely to be persecuted then?'

'Nup.'

'That tattooed fella did, though, didn't he?'

'What?'

'Got persecuted!'

Lightning Strikes

When the lighting struck, it was unexpected. There was a loud crack, a burst of flame and then a smell of burning.

Tom Gardner was in a panic. The storm had been one of the worst he had encountered for many a year and he had seen the lightning from the kitchen window, zigzagging down towards the paddock. So as soon as the worst of it was over, he rushed out to inspect his precious hives. The bees were a big part of his life and he kept them in a secure part of his small farm.

His heart sank as he turned the key in the padlock and opened the gate. There were dead bees everywhere on the ground and the rest were panicking and swarming, and he realised he should have put his protective gear on.

'Gonna get stung,' he muttered. 'Wonder where the queen's got to.'

He inspected the damaged hives. Two were totally shattered and the remaining one just broken a little on one side. I could fix that one up, no worries, he thought.

Tom's feet stuck to the ground where honey had seeped out of the broken combs and he groaned as he saw all his profit from the latest batch disappearing into the mud.

Surprisingly, though, the bees were making no attempt to attack.

Perhaps they know it's me, he thought. Do bees recognise people? he wondered. Tom had been looking after his bees for many years. He talked to them; sometimes he played his music on the little radio he kept in the shed.

Then he saw a queen. She was sitting still, on top of the partially damaged hive. He knew she was looking at him as he moved towards her and still she didn't budge.

'Come on then, my beauty,' he muttered and raised his arm, then watched, transfixed, as she flew up and rested on the back of his hand.

Then the rest of the bees gathered together, calmer now, and proceeded to settle on the ground next to the damaged hive. Tom slowly lowered his hand, then the queen flew off and disappeared into the middle of her faithful subjects.

Tom hurried over to his tool shed and grabbed a piece of timber some nails, hammer and a saw and went over to mend the broken hive. It was easily fixed. He pulled away the damaged timber, sawed the end of the piece he had brought to replace it with and nailed it over the hole. Then he looked at the honeycombs inside. They all seemed to be intact and he breathed a sigh of relief.

He looked down at the bees, who were huddled together and appeared to be sitting patiently, waiting for instructions.

'Come on then,' he said now as he opened the top of the repaired hive. 'You'll all have to share the same space for a while until I can get the other hives fixed up.'

Then he watched anxiously as the queen separated herself from the rest then flew into the hive. Gradually, the others followed until they had all disappeared, the angry buzzing now reduced to a low comforting hum.

Old Tom stood for a moment, then, shaking his head in disbelief but with a big smile on his face, went back indoors and started cooking his tea.

Crossroads

It was a dilemma. Marg didn't know what to do. They had told her to turn left at the crossroads. The first crossroads she had turned left at about half an hour ago had led nowhere, a dead end to a paddock. Would this be the right one? She gazed anxiously around. There were no signs, except…hang on, she thought, what was that? She put the car in park and went over to the other side of the road.

There was a signpost lying on the ground. 'Allaboraboo', it said. She lifted it up and tried to work out which way it had been pointing. At least it was where she was headed. Allaboraboo. She remembered the argument back at the service station when they gave her directions.

'If you're coming from the south then you turn right,' he had said, but then the old Aboriginal bloke had said, 'No, you turn left if you're coming from the south, and if you're coming from the east you go straight over.'

'The same if you're coming from the north,' the other one had said, and nodded, 'then you go straight over.'

Marg pondered. She hadn't really understood any of the directions. She had been headed north, at least she had thought she had, but now she remembered that when she had taken the wrong turn last time she had turned off onto another track which had led her back to another bitumen road and she had thought she was back on the main road. But maybe she wasn't. This signpost could have been on any one of these roads.

Marg sighed and went back to the car. She reached for her phone to try again for the farmhouse where she was meant to be staying. She didn't know too much about Allaboraboo, just that it was a small community and the school was used by children from local families and farmers. Also it had been a rush job. The local schoolteacher had been taken ill and Marg was filling in for as long as they needed her.

She consulted her map again. There were so many tracks that were just not marked and she couldn't even place where she was at the moment. The GPS had packed up just past Bendigo.

There was no sound from the phone. No dialling tone. She checked the battery level. There was still some time left; she had made sure she had charged it up before leaving. She threw the phone back into her bag and reached for her bottle of water, which was now almost empty, and realised she should have got another one back at the service station. It had been nearly forty degrees today. Thank goodness the car's air conditioner was working, she thought.

She looked at her watch again. It would be dusk soon. How come there's no traffic, she wondered. At least I could get directions if I could stop someone. Until now, Marg hadn't been too worried. She liked the outdoors, the outback. She had worked in country schools before as a substitute teacher, and as a rule she didn't get stressed about getting lost, which she had to admit she frequently did, but there was always someone to help you on your way.

But now for the first time, she felt the beginnings of panic; she could be stranded here all night. But they were expecting her weren't they, she told herself, perhaps somebody would come and look for her. She could stay here and wait for someone to come along. But what if no one came? All these thoughts were milling around her head when common sense took over.

She got out of the car again and squinted at the sun, which was, she reckoned, about twenty minutes from the horizon. In the west. Obvious. She turned around and faced east. Then she realised: her car was facing east, the sun had been behind her, she had been driving east. She had to get back onto the main road going north.

Mentally berating herself for her stupidity, Marg got back into the car again and turned left. Hopefully, I'm on the right track now, she thought, this must be north, gotta be there soon, and she increased speed as she turned the radio on. But surprise, surprise, there was no reception, just static. So she sat in silence looking in vain for a left turn. There were no signs of habitation and not one vehicle visible in the distance in either direction.

She had been driving for about ten minutes when more doubts started to creep in. She thought back again. She had to drive north and then look for a sign on the left to Allaboraboo. If this place was so far from the last crossing, why then had the broken road sign been so far away?

It was quickly getting darker now, the sky turning from orange red to a beautiful deep purple; she loved these outback sunsets.

Marg checked the petrol gauge again. Nearly half a tank. Should be heaps to get me there, she was thinking, so was deep in thought when suddenly the car rocked as something hit it violently on the passenger side, and she watched in horror as the window cracked and something big slid down out of sight. She stepped on the brake and stopped, heart pounding.

As soon as she could stop shaking, Marg went around to the other side of the car. She had guessed what it was: a kangaroo had appeared from out of nowhere and hit the car. It happened, she knew, but it had never happened to her before.

The animal was lying on the ground, blood pouring from its head. It was huge, a beautiful grey-blue. Its eyes were wide open, staring, vacant, lifeless. She realised it was dead and tears were welling in pity for the death of such a beautiful animal. She could do nothing except move it to the side of the road out of the way.

It was only as she tried to grab its legs that she noticed the pouch and the tiny leg sticking out.

'Oh no!' Marg gasped and moved closer. It was hard to see. The light was almost gone and she opened the car door again and searched in the glovebox for the torch. Gently she grasped the Joey's leg and manoeuvred it out from the pouch. It was alive. About thirty centimetres long, she guessed, bright eyes open, looking at her.

There was a blanket on the back seat and, quickly pulling it out, Marg wrapped it around the small creature, cuddling it to herself for a moment before putting it carefully onto the passenger seat. She was so totally engrossed that she hadn't noticed the ute pulling up across the road, and turned around in surprise as a tall figure wearing a big hat suddenly appeared from behind her car.

'Gooday,' boomed a large voice. 'Howyagoing?'

She turned, tears still in her eyes looking up at a big red beard. 'Um, hi,' she managed. ' I've hit a kangaroo and there's a joey,' she said. 'I've put it in a blanket, and I'm going to Allaboraboo. I got lost for a bit but can you tell me if I'm on the right road now?' It all came out in a rush as she wiped the tears from her eyes on her sleeve.

The big voice was gentle now. 'I reckon you must be Marg.' He put out his hand. 'I'm Dave,' he said. 'They sent me out to look for you.'

Marg, overwhelmed with relief, managed a smile and shook his hand. He walked around the car, looked at the kangaroo and, seemingly with no effort at all, pulled it off to the side of the road, then he examined the crack in the glass.

He looked at Marg closely. 'Looks like you had a bit of a fright,' he said. 'She must have given that window a heck of a whack. Tell you what,' he added, 'how about we grab your bags, and I'll drive you up to the farmhouse. It's only a couple of ks. We can collect your car in the morning.'

He was taking charge, much to Marg's relief. So she opened the boot and handed him her bags, which he put into the back of the ute, then settled herself on the front seat as he carefully passed her the baby roo.

He laid his hand on the blanket into which the joey had completely disappeared. 'Don't worry about him,' he said. 'The kids're used to looking after joeys. They'll turn him into a pet most likely.'

The left turn turned out to be only a short distance away and in the dim light Marg could just make out the road sign for Allaboraboo. Then as the twinkling lights from the homestead appeared, she finally relaxed.

She could feel the Joey moving around under the blanket and patted it gently.

'You OK, Marg?' Dave's voice was kind, concerned.

'I'm fine,' she said.

Shaggy Dog Story

Maggy sighed as her husband Barty launched into his party piece. She had heard the same joke so many times before, she almost couldn't bear to hear it again. They were on holiday in Tasmania and the other people on their tour hadn't heard it, so Barty was taking full advantage of a captive audience. He had as usual partaken of quite a few beers and she had tried to tell him to slow down but they had all been telling jokes and of course he couldn't resist.

'I know a good one,' he had said. It was a shaggy dog story about a mean man who had expected his wife to buy a lottery ticket, which involved all sorts of problems with a lost credit card and various prolonged traumas. He had got to the part where the man on the TV was calling out the winning numbers when Barty paused and said, 'And you'll never guess what happened next.'

There was silence then and Maggie looked up as she waited for the punchline.

'Well, go on, finish it then,' said Bob the bartender. 'What happened next?'

Barty always liked to make a dramatic pause before the ending but this time the silence was more prolonged than usual and then Maggie watched in horror as Barty clutched his chest and fell to the floor.

Well, of course the holiday was cut short. Barty's long-overdue heart attack had been fatal and Maggie had to deal with getting his body back home and cope with the funeral and so on. The children helped and his life insurance policy was substantial, so Maggie got on with her life as best she could. She had kept in touch with friends she had made on the Tassie tour, though, and one day she had an email from Bob the bartender. It was a friendly letter hoping she was well and inviting her to travel back and finish the tour of the area which had been cut short, due to Barty's sad demise. She was welcome to stay at the hotel, he said, which he now owned.

'Go on, Mum, go,' encouraged Shirl, the oldest. 'You need a break. Go and have a good time,'

So she did. She booked the flight and sent a letter to Bob, who said he would meet her at the airport.

It all went very well. In fact, so well that Maggie found herself having such a good time enjoying Bob's company and loving Tassie so much that her stay went on for quite a long while.

One day when they were having a nice candlelit dinner at a quiet table in Bob's hotel, he asked what he had been wanting to ask for a long while. 'Can I ask you something, Maggie?' he said.

'Of course, anything. What is it?' She felt a little flutter of excitement and looked up at him, expectant, secretly hoping what he might be going to ask.

'Well,' Bob started, 'it's about that joke Barty was telling when he, you know, had his heart attack.'

Maggie looked confused. This was a bit strange. 'Um, yes,' she said.

'Well, he never got to finish it and I've been wondering, you know, what the ending was. Do you remember?'

He waited then while Maggie composed her face and got her thoughts together. As if she would ever forget!

'Yes, I know the ending,' she said.

Bob looked excited and leaned forward over the table. So she told him about the winning numbers coming up, that the man had died of a heart attack, and his wife had all the money to herself.

Bob laughed. 'Well, that was a good ending. Thanks for telling me. It's been bugging me ever since. So Maggie, you know how the tourists like to hear a good yarn over a beer or two, so do you mind if I use Barty's joke? I have an idea how I could alter it a bit to make it even better.'

Of course she didn't mind, even if the question he had asked wasn't the one she had expected. 'Sure, Bob, no worries,' she said.

So the next time a group of tourists were staying and someone started telling yarns, Bob leaned over the bar. 'I know a good one,' he said. He looked over at Maggie sitting in the corner and winked. 'This is a true story,' he said. 'There was a bloke called Barty who was staying here in this hotel who liked to tell a good yarn and told this one about a nasty kind of a guy who liked to buy lottery tickets.'

Bob went through the whole rigmarole until he came to the part where Barty had said, 'Guess what happened next.'

'Guess what happened next,' repeated Bob.

'What?' they chorused.

'Nobody found out,' said Bob, ' because before he could finish the story, he had a heart attack and died.'

The confused discussion that followed led to many more beers being consumed and Bob had a big smile on his face. Maggie had a moment's unease over the way the story had been turned around and Barty being involved, but she had to admit it had been a good yarn, so she let it pass. She was happy here in this place, Bob was a kind, loving man, they were happy together and so she stayed.

It was five years later. Maggie was helping out in the bar and talking to the tourists when as usual someone started telling stories. She sighed as Bob launched into his party piece. She had heard the same story now for so any times and now she almost couldn't bear to hear it again.

'I know a good one,' said Bob.

Maggie looked at him as he launched into 'This is a true story about a bloke called Barty,' and she noted his expanding waistline, his balding hair and his red face. He loved to have a beer with his guests and she had tried to tell him to ease up, but he wouldn't listen. 'You worry too much,' he had told her. 'I'm fine, everything's fine.'

Guess what happened next!

The Apple

Gerald regarded the apple with suspicion.

He glanced over at the assortment of fifteen-year-olds. They were milling around, chattering, laughing, shouting. They hadn't settled down yet after the lunch break, the noise was overwhelming and he was getting a headache.

Who, he wondered, had put that apple on his desk. Someone's idea of a joke was it? None of these kids would do it for any other reason, he decided. Sometimes he wondered what he was doing here. He used to enjoy teaching once back in the day, when they did what they were told, had respect, actually learned something and did homework.

Gerald cleared his throat. 'Quieten down,' he shouted, 'and get to your seats.' He had to shout or they ignored him, which was what they were doing now in any case.

He opened his desk drawer and pulled out the little hammer that he had brought from home. He banged it hard three times on the desk and then watched as they took their time getting to their desks, and he waited, eyeing each one of them, still wondering about the apple.

There were twelve girls and thirteen boys in his geography class. Most of them didn't want to be there – they considered geography a waste of time – and yet he knew that one day they would travel. They would explore the world; they all did nowadays. He hoped that today's lesson about Indonesia would whet their appetites for a little more knowledge about one of our closest neighbours.

It did, to a degree. Later on, when he asked them who had actually been to Indonesia, some of them put their hands up. It quietened down when they started with the test paper and map drawings and Gerald set-tled back in his seat, once again contemplating the puzzle of the apple.

It had to be a girl, hadn't it? Surely none of the boys would ever present him with an apple; they'd be a laughing stock if the others found out. He thought again about it being a joke. He knew he wasn't the sort of teacher one would play a joke on – they thought he didn't have a sense of humour. Actually he did, he liked a joke, but they didn't know that, which was fine by him. He knew they referred to him as Mr Grumpy, which he knew he was; it was the only way he could teach. If he tried to be nice, which he did once, they started taking advantage. One of them even called him by his Christian name of Gerald, instead of Sir, and that certainly wouldn't do; familiarity breeds contempt, was his opinion. He was not their friend or their brother or substitute father, he was their teacher.

He wondered whether he should ask them. 'Who does this apple belong to?' he could say, and see if anyone put their hand up; of course no one would, would they?

So Gerald started looking over the girls. There was Mary Dougal sitting in the front seat. A pretty curly-haired blonde, one of the few girls who actually seemed to enjoy his class and handed in her homework each day with a shy little smile and barely spoke a word. No, Gerald decided, she wouldn't be brave enough to leave an apple on his desk

He looked at Shelley seated one row behind. A cheeky fifteen-year-old going on twenty-five. Dark hair. Very attractive. Sometimes she eyed him in a way that made him feel slightly uncomfortable. She looked up just then and caught him staring. She stared back, big brown eyes challenging, mocking yet inviting. Gerald looked away quickly.

He contemplated the apple again and wondered. An unwanted unaccustomed feeling swept over him. Did Shelley actually think that he liked her? Was she playing some sort of game? What was she up to? He thought he knew now who must have put the apple there. He looked at her again. Her eyes were still settled on him. Then she glanced at the apple and smiled at him knowingly as she bent to her work again.

Gerald found himself feeling just a little bit flattered. Totally ridiculous. Yet he couldn't help himself looking at her school shirt, unbuttoned down as far as it could decently go. She was well built, he noticed, compared to many of the other girls her age.

Gerald could feel his face going red and shook his head trying to clear unwanted thoughts, then turned towards the classroom door as there was a gentle knock and the Art teacher Jeff Batts poked his head round.

He looked over to Gerald then flung the door open and crossed over to his desk. 'Sorry to barge in.' he said. 'I'm wondering if you have my apple.' He looked around. 'Ah, there it is!' he exclaimed as he reached over and picked it up from Gerald's desk, threw it up into the air and then caught it again. 'One of my lot left it here,' he said. 'He got the wrong room. This is part of a still life I'm trying to organise for the next session.' He gave a half wave as he left the room. 'Thanks for looking after it for me.'

The bell went then and they all started packing things away.

'Leave your exercise books on my desk on your way out,' Gerald told them, then shouted, 'and don't forget to do your homework.'

The Teacher

The boy's laughter was contagious and they all started giggling, which turned into full-blown guffaws ringing around the classroom as they ran around throwing screwed-up pieces of paper to one another.

'Quiet!' a thunderous voice boomed, and they all turned to look at the large bearded man standing in the classroom doorway, a grim expression on his face as he strode across the floor to his desk. He glowered at the unruly year sevens and stared at them until they quietened. 'Resume your seats,' he barked.

They sat down then, not a little intimidated by his formidable presence, and they waited. He looked them over one by one and it was clear that he didn't much like what he saw. There was a malevolent look in his eyes which were dark and penetrating and he glared at Garry, who had been responsible for the bad joke which had started then all off laughing. The boy held the teacher's eye for a moment and a wave of unaccountable fear coursed through his body. He shivered as he quickly looked down at his desk.

'I am your teacher for today.' The man's voice was quieter now, but still menacing. 'You will call me Sir, there will be no talking. If you have a specific question relating to the subject of the lesson, you may raise your hand. If anyone attempts to use a mobile phone, it will be confiscated.' He regarded them all intently again. 'Is that clear?' he asked. Nobody responded. 'Is that clear?' he thundered.

The response was quick this time. 'Yes, sir!' they chorused, albeit some of them half-heartedly, then they kept quiet and watched as he pulled a book out of a big black bag.

'Get out your maths book. You are going to learn basic algebra today.' He turned towards the whiteboard and his shoulders stiffened

for a moment as someone let out a loud groan. They all held their breath
as they waited for him to turn around again but to their relief he kept
on writing.

The class was unusually quiet as they sat through the lesson, wrote
in exercise books and tried to understand what he was talking about,
and they also kept quiet when he asked if there were any questions.
When the bell for recess went, they all filed out quietly.

'You must have put the fear of God into those kids, Nick,' remarked
Harry, the principal, who had been watching them all leave. 'I've never
seen them go so quietly before. No one else has been able to handle the
high jinks of that wild bunch.

The malevolent look had turned benign as Nick Parker smiled. 'The
fear of God doesn't cut it with some kids,' he said.

Then he turned away and, for a brief moment, his eyes darkened to
coal-black and the whites glared red, then they cleared and the benign
look was back.

The Dunny

'Wake up, Nan.' A small gentle hand was patting my arm. 'I think we're nearly there.'

I opened my eyes. 'I wasn't asleep,' I said. 'I was just resting my eyes.'

In fact, I had been remembering what it was like in this place about forty years ago. I was around thirty at the time. Young, strong and looking forward to a new life on a farm in outback South Australia.

We had bought the old homestead and a huge piece of land, and that day we had arrived with a trailer full of stuff ahead of the removal van which was bringing the rest of the furniture.

The farmhouse needed fixing up, the previous elderly owner had passed away and the place had not been lived in for a couple of years. There was a lot of repairing and renovating to do and the building was in a generally bad state of repair, which was why we had got it so cheap. There was no mains water, just the big water tank, no electricity, and the old wood stove looked as though it would be a challenge to say the least. This was all a formidable prospect but all doable.

But I hadn't even considered the toilet. We had looked again through the house making notes of what needed fixing when it suddenly occurred to me. 'Where's the dunny?' I asked him who had been so keen on this project and professed to be able to use his carpenter skills to be able to make or fix up anything.

He looked a bit sheepish. 'Um,' he said, 'I thought you knew. It's outside.' H pointed to the back door, which was half off its hinges.

Suddenly anxious, I went out and looked around. At first, I could see nothing which resembled a toilet and I took a few paces into the scrubby bush, kicking my way through the golden sand. Then I saw it, about thirty paces away, barely visible and surrounded by small gum trees.

My heart sank. It was bad enough that the house was in so much bad repair and that there was so much work to do, but to have to walk all the way out here to go to the toilet was almost more than I could bear. As I drew closer, I saw a small corrugated-iron shed, with a roof tilted over onto one side of the structure that was leaning so far over you would wonder why it didn't completely collapse. I walked carefully round to the other side.

There was no door. I looked inside and gazed in amazement at a four-gallon drum wedged into the sand with an old wooden toilet seat perched on the top. Cautiously, I edged closer and peered into a hole. It seemed to be very deep and there was all sorts of debris, rubbish, twigs, leaves and old cans almost reaching the top. Then I jumped back in horror as a large spider appeared from under the toilet seat and, in my haste to leave, tripped and fell down outside. This was the last straw. I feared spiders.

For a few minutes, I stayed there, sitting on the warm sand. I thought about all the work to be done, which I had more or less resigned myself to, but this? How could I manage three children with the youngest not even toilet-trained? It was suddenly all so overwhelming, I just sat there on the warm sand, and my eyes filled with tears.

It took a little while but then I pulled myself together and walked back to the house. He must have seen the look on my face.

'Don't worry,' he said, 'I'll fix it up, no worries.'

Which he did, eventually. Some planks of wood formed a built-in bench with a neat little hole in the top. The walls were reinforced with readily available timber, the roof firmly put back into place and the corrugated iron painted green, the path was cleared with everyone helping, mallee stumps removed and piled up ready to be chopped for burning. All the spiders had been removed and everything sprayed.

The hole was cleaned out and dug deeper. When it was all finished, I was so happy to be rid of the buckets and potties that everyone had been using. So we had a proper long-drop at last but it was still scary to go out there at night, with just a torch, or even carrying a kerosene lamp. It was always so dark, and I was always worried about spiders even though I knew they had all gone.

Daytime wasn't so bad, though. Sometimes I would just sit in there in quiet contemplation and leave the door open, gazing north into the bush, which just kept going hundred of kilometres into the distance. It was a strangely calming sort of serendipity.

I was lost in thought again when I heard a small impatient voice say, 'Come on, Nan, are you coming?'

The overseas visitors who we had brought up here to see where we used to live on the farm were exclaiming with delight. 'Oh how beautiful it is,' they were saying. 'How you must have loved living here!'

I wasn't surprised to see that the old farmhouse had disappeared. There was a concrete patch left where the floor of the main room had been. Strong winds and dust storms had probably seen to that I thought, or scavengers looking for iron and timber.

My granddaughter was pointing towards the bush where something glistened in the scrub. 'What's that over there, Nan?' she asked.

I shaded my eyes. 'I reckon that's the old dunny,' I said, not quite believing what I was seeing.

We walked over there carefully, kicking the golden sand, which was just as I remembered it, and watching for snakes.

It was still there. The long-drop, still standing after all these years. We peeked inside. Even the bench was still intact, although the hole was filled with all sorts of rubbish.

'Did you used to go to the toilet here then, Nan?' There was awe in her voice, wonder in her eyes. I nodded, unable to voice the memories flooding back.

'Do you remember that from a long time ago then?'

'Yes, sweetheart, I remember,' I said.

Bali Impressions

Outside our holiday apartments are four lounge chairs facing the pool, which is about ten paces away over beautifully manicured grass. I am watching a Balinese boy mow the same piece of grass for the second time.

It's not quite so humid today. The air is warm, the sky blue, and a gentle breeze moves the palm fronds around.

'Hello, *Mem*,' says a voice behind me. It is the young man who has been tidying the room.

I turn and he smiles.

'*Mem* happy?' he asks.

'Yes, happy, thank you,' I reply.

Then he leaves, looking very pleased with himself.

I hear the sound of snipping scissors and see another boy (or younger man – it's difficult to tell ages). He is clipping the edges with large scissors. I watch as another boy approaches, squats down alongside the younger one and appears to be giving him lessons on how to use the scissors. Apparently it is not being done correctly.

They both sit and chat for a while, then smile and part amicably. The younger man unhurriedly proceeds with the work in precisely the same way as before.

This is typical of Bali behaviour. No fuss. No hurry. Everything will be done eventually with a smile.

These are gentle, quietly spoken people. Very friendly and polite to the hotel guests, but still dignified and never subservient.

Everyone seems to be employed, doing something around the resort to keep the apartments, gardens and pools in pristine condition.

I watched yesterday in amazement as a few boys with long-handled brushes actually swept the sand on the beach, getting rid of the very small pieces of rubbish gathered during the past few hours. Then more boys arrived with spades – I counted ten – as they proceeded to dig sand from the beach and then throw it into the sea. Apparently, as I discovered later, they are trying to extend the beach. The water in the bay here appears to be calm, with no waves to stir things around too much. Just as well, I suppose, or this would all be a wasted effort.

Visiting Europeans with loud voices and noisy children spoil the tranquillity of this place for a little while, then they are gone and peace is restored.

This morning, I nearly stepped on what I thought was rubbish. It's a good job I missed, because around the ground in various spots, and in little temples, hand-built, are small offerings for the Hindu spirits. They bring good luck and keep this a happy place. It seems that most Balinese families have their own temple at home. I have a great respect for people's culture and customs and if this is what is responsible for the tranquillity of this place, then it's certainly working.

We have a Balinese driver named Kadek. A friendly soul who has lived here all of his life and knows all the good places to go. Yesterday we went for a drive. I was interested in seeing some of the countryside, but wasn't prepared for the numbers of scooters, cars and general chaos of traffic everywhere. The number of people able to get on a bike is outstanding. Mum, Dad and one, two, or even three children all squashed up together. They zip in and out between cars and pedestrians, sometimes so close it is scary. Bike helmets are not compulsory, but a lot of people wear them by choice. Some are nicely decorated in their own individual way.

Everyone politely makes way for everyone else. There is no finger pointing, name calling or obscenities shouted out in anger. There is an occasional polite short horn toot, mainly to let people know you are coming, and not to let someone know they have done something stupid!

The cars pass one another on very narrow streets with an infinitesimal space between. Buses also somehow get into the action, squeezing into the limited space. Traffic is held up while all the manoeuvring is done. It seems to be a strangely orchestrated organisation out of seemingly absolute mayhem. I likened it to being in the middle of a ballet dance with everyone flying around and narrowly escaping actually knocking into anybody else.

Also, strangely, all the vehicles looked clean, shiny, scratch and bump free.

The ride in Kadek's nice clean shiny air-conditioned car was one of the most hair-raising experiences of my life. There are seat belts fitted in the front for the driver and passenger, but none at the back. Seat belts are not compulsory in Bali. Most of the roads are in very poor condition, and whoever is sitting the back of the car gets bounced around a fair bit.

Speed limits are ignored, although with the amount of traffic it would be hard to go more than forty ks at most, except when we eventually got on to the main highway to go north to visit a Temple Lake. Then Kadek put his foot down and drove right in the centre of the road, moving only to avoid oncoming traffic. He told us that the police do not concern themselves with traffic infringements. In fact, I saw very few police. I did see one at a crossroads once, who had a whistle which he blew vigorously, but no one was paying any attention.

I asked Kadek what would happen if there was an accident. He said they would never call the police. Any bumps or dents would be fixed up by the owners or their friends. There is no comprehensive Insurance. Mobile phones seem to be plentiful. There are teenagers on scooters, and drivers in cars, all texting and phoning while driving.

I watched Kadek take a call. Phone in right hand, left hand on steering wheel. He had to use the clutch, so the car moved forward with no hands on the wheel while he changed gears, and texted a message at the same time. We told him what would happen if a policeman caught him doing that in Australia and he laughed. What would be a big deal to us is not even worth worrying about in Bali.

The lawn tidiers are back. They have already been once today. They are busy in a non-hurried way with long-handled brushes as they gather up leaves which have fallen from the various trees during the past couple of hours. This is never ending work, as is that of the pool cleaner, a young Javanese fellow who does both jobs. He is a bright intelligent boy who works from six a.m. till two p.m. He is learning the Balinese language, speaks fairly good English and loves chatting with the tourists. His prospects of advancement are very poor, but he, like his Balinese friends, is happy, likes his work and doesn't worry at all about the future.

There are three pools, always sparking clean and kept in pristine condition. They are warm enough from the sun's rays to enjoy a dip anytime of the day or night.

I am being called for lunch and we walk about thirty paces to the outdoor restaurant, where there is a choice of beautifully cooked Asian or European food. Served quickly, efficiently with a smile. I try to remember the Balinese word for thank you that I learned yesterday.

The lovely young waitress gives me a smile.

We have lunch. Today, no one is thinking about the future.

Everyone is happy.

Paving Stones

It had been a regular routine for the past five years. Drive to the station, park the car and catch the train to the city, then a five-minute walk to his office. Malcom was a creature of habit. He liked routine, where everything was comfortable, predictable and probably what some people would consider to be boring. But it was Malcom's life and he was OK with that.

So when one morning the car wouldn't start, Malcolm was thrown into an unfamiliar state of anxiety and indecision. He soon realised that due to the rain on his way home yesterday, he had turned the car lights on, then had been in a hurry to get indoors and forgotten to turn them off. The battery was old and now it was flat.

Malcom was flustered. He prided himself on always being on time for work, and if he waited for the RAA to come, he would be late. He looked at his watch. He was always early for the train and the station was about one and a half kilometres away, so he decided, if he walked quickly enough he could maybe make it, then he could call the RAA when he arrived home tonight. There was always a bus, he thought and the stop was much closer than the train, but he didn't know how often they ran and the thought of waiting for a bus for an unknown amount of time sent him into a quiet panic.

So Malcom made the decision. He closed the garage door again and for the third time checked that the front and screen doors were locked, then, briefcase in hand, determination on his face, he started walking along the street to the main road.

Every Saturday, he walked to the shops and knew exactly how many paving stones there were along his road and up to the corner. Today was no different and he started counting as usual, with the first one which was in line with his front gate and up to the end where they stopped, and the pavement joined with the main road, which was concrete. He had counted them many times but he always had to count them again whenever he went along the street, just to make sure that nothing had changed.

He tried to walk quickly and kept his head down as he counted aloud, each stride exactly the same width as the pavers, which made it easier to keep track. He didn't notice the occasional curious stares of the morning dog walkers. It was only when he arrived at the main road that he realised with dismay he had only counted eighty-seven and he knew for a fact there should have been ninety-three.

Malcolm was panting a little; he had been walking as fast as he could, his portly frame not quite used to this unaccustomed exercise, and desperately trying to remember what could have been different, how he could have miscounted. He looked wildly around and back along the road. He wanted so badly to go and count them again but there wasn't time, he had to get to the station.

It was hard to keep walking with the worry of the paving stones at the back of his mind, so he didn't really notice the time passing, although when he reached the station he still hadn't walked quickly enough, because just as he arrived he saw the train leaving.

Malcolm paced agitatedly up and down the platform. He eyed the seat just outside the waiting room. It looked little grubby, plus there were puddles from the rain. He was fastidious about his clothes. His suit which he always wore to work was always neatly pressed, his shoes polished. He decided not to risk sitting down and carefully avoided getting his shoes muddy.

The trains arrived every twenty minutes to go to the city, so there wasn't really long to wait, but for Malcolm it was an eternity. and when he finally arrived and had walked to his building, he was nearly half an hour late.

No one was in the lift when he went up to the third floor to his office. He tried to get to his cubicle as quickly as possible, hoping he hadn't been missed, but no one gave him a second glance and he sank down on his familiar chair with a relieved sigh.

'You OK, Malcolm?' It was Mary, the office manager. She had suddenly appeared by his side, looking a little anxious. 'I was worried about you,' she said.

He was aware of the concern in her voice as he regarded with satisfaction the pile of invoices and the receipt books stacked in the in tray waiting for his attention. Then he frowned as he noticed the neatly painted wooden sign on his desk with the words Accountant and, underneath, his name Malcolm Muggridge. It had been moved from its position where he kept it, exactly in line with the out tray on the right-hand side of his desk. He wondered if the cleaners had done it on purpose. Mary waited as he reached over and carefully placed the sign back in position.

Malcolm stared at the green button on her cardigan. He had a problem with looking at people's eyes, then he replied in his quiet voice, 'I had a flat battery,' he said. 'I missed the train. I'm sorry I'm late.'

He didn't tell her about the paving stones. He would count them again tonight on his way home and, with that comforting thought in mind, he turned the computer on.

Mary regarded him kindly and he flinched a little as she patted him on his shoulder, 'Just so long as you're OK, Malcolm,' she said.

Mirabel

My best friend is called Marcia. I have lots of brothers and sisters, so our house is quite crowded and nobody notices whether I am at home or not, and there are not enough toys to go around, plus there aren't any books. Marcia doesn't have any brothers or sisters and she has lots of toys and books, but nobody to talk to, which is why I spend a lot of time at Marcia's place and then she is not so lonely. We play games and have lots of fun.

Marcia's mum doesn't really notice me except when she calls out to her and says, 'Who are you talking to, Marcia?' and then Marcia says, 'It's my friend Mirabel. She's come to borrow a book.'

Sometimes I stay over for tea and then Marcia's mum makes sure she puts an extra plate out for me.

So everything was fine and dandy until one day when we were playing a game and Marcia's mum calls out for her to come downstairs as she wants her to meet somebody.

'You'd better stay here,' Marcia said, so I stayed in her room for a little while and then I got curious and went to have a look over the banister.

There was another girl there, and Marcia's mum was saying, 'Lucy has come to play with you. She's our new next-door neighbour and she has no friends, o how about you take her upstairs to see your room?'

Then they start coming up the stairs and I wasn't too happy about that. Marcia and I were in the middle of a game and, worst of all, Marcia said to me in a whisper so Lucy couldn't hear, 'You'd better go now Mirabel. I'll see you tomorrow.'

So I went, but when I came back the next day, to my amazement, there was Lucy again, and Marcia completely ignored me as if I wasn't there, so I had to go home again.

This was very hurtful, so I had to make a plan.

I watched as all the children lined up on the pavement next day after school to wait for the school bus. Marcia didn't even see me. She hadn't even spoken to me at school either. Anyway, just as the bus got there I got behind Lucy, who was standing right in the front of the queue, and quickly gave her a great big push. She fell right in front of the bus, which only just managed to stop before it went right over the top of her.

Of course there was a lot of shouting and crying and the ambulance came. I thought that perhaps she was dead, but she wasn't. Anyway, I think she'll be in hospital for a long time.

So now things are back to normal for a while and I can go and play with Marcia again.

Her mum still calls out, 'Who are you talking to, Marcia?'

You'd think she'd be used to me by now, wouldn't you?

Pungo's World

Pungo lived with his dad Pongo and his mum Mongo in a mud hut up in the mountains, far away from other people. He often wondered about the world he lived in and many times asked his dad what lay beyond the far horizon.

'That, my son,' said Pongo, 'is the edge of the world.'

'But how do ou know?' asked Pungo.

His dad told him of the many stories handed down from his forefathers. How the world was flat, and that if you went to the edge of the world, you would drop off into space and join the stars you could see in the night sky.

One day when Pungo was fourteen years old and grown-up, his curiosity got the better of him and he told his mother and father he was going away to see for himself what it was like at the edge of the world.

Pongo told him to be careful and gave his son a bow and arrow and a newly made club to defend himself from wild animals. Pungo set off, feeling very excited to be going on his first journey alone.

He headed down the mountain towards the horizon, but all that day as he travelled, he never came to the end of the track. Occasionally he would meet a wild goat, or a pig, and there were many rocks which he had to clamber over. Sometimes he would climb to the top of a high one to see if he could see the end of the world but all he could see were more rocks.

That night he found a place to sleep in a cave and thought to himself, tomorrow, I will come to the edge of the world. But the next day was the same. The horizon stretched further and further away and again Pungo had to find somewhere to rest. He killed birds to eat and ate berries and roots.

On the third day, to Pungo's delight, he thought he saw the end getting near, and then discovered that the track had finally disappeared. The rocks had been getting smaller and smaller, the trees fewer and he came to a grassy plain which seemed to suddenly stop.

As he came closer and closer to the end, he fell down onto his belly and crawled carefully towards the edge. He slowly peeped over the top, expecting to see nothing but space.

But what he saw filled him with amazement. There far below him at the bottom of the hill was sand and then water. Lots of water, as far as his eyes could see. Pungo had only seen water from the rain falling into puddles, and there was water in the ground up in the mountains which they had to drink. There were small waterfalls and sometimes the rain made a little lake, but this sight of so much water stretching so far away was beyond his imagination.

Another wondrous thing that he could now see was something floating on the water. It looked like a big house with many holes along the sides, and there were people walking on the top and all around on it. Pungo sat and watched for a long time.

He noticed the water house getting bigger. It was coming closer to the land below the cliff where Pungo was hiding behind some bushes. Excitement was building in all his body as he saw the strange clothes the people were wearing, nothing like the animal skins which he had wrapped around himself.

He watched transfixed then as some of the people climbed down from the big water house onto another smaller one which started to come towards the sand at the bottom of the cliff where he was watching.

Pungo's first thought was to quickly make his way back home, before any of the strange-looking people could see him, and maybe punish him for spying on them. He couldn't wait to tell his father what the edge of the world was really like, but his curiosity was even greater than his fear of the unknown, and he wanted a closer look, so he slowly edged over the top of the cliff onto the sand. Trying not to make himself seen, he carefully crawled down the steep hill, hiding where he could among the grass and shrubs growing in the sandy dunes.

But then, in spite of his care, Pungo suddenly lost his footing and slipped and, to his terror, started rolling down and down. Head over heels. He couldn't stop. Desperately, he tried to grab onto tufts of grass, but the momentum of the fall was too strong.

Sore and shaken, he finally came to a halt, covered in sand. He slowly opened his eye,s which he'd closed in fright, and blinked up at the tall figure of a young man who was gazing down at him with amazement.

He recoiled and tried to wriggle backwards as a hand reached towards him and the stranger spoke to him in a foreign tongue. His voice was gentle and his eyes were kind so that Pungo didn't feel quite so afraid any more, and he took the stranger's hand, who helped him up.

Pungo pulled his goatskin back around himself where it had come adrift, got to his feet and tried to brush the sand away. Then he stood as straight and tall as he could, although even then he only reached as high as the stranger's shoulder.

He smiled his beautiful Pungo smile and gave a little bow, which was the traditional custom when friends greeted friends from another tribe. The tall man smiled back and, putting his arm across Pungo's shoulder, led him towards the boat, now fully come to rest on the sand.

Men and women were disembarking and quickly gathered around and stood staring at Pungo in surprise. He felt shy and embarrassed at first, being the centre of attention of all these strange people, but then, as he saw the friendly looks and smiles, he became more comfortable, and confident.

A young man, about the same size as Pungo drew closer. He lifted a corner of the goatskin around the boy's body and stroked it with admiring looks. 'What animal is this?' he asked.

Pungo looked bewildered. He had no idea what the person was saying. But he understood that he liked his goatskin and pointed to it. Goomba' he said.

'Goomba?' The man repeated the word and Pungo smiled and nodded.

He wondered why all these people had white skin. Pungo had chocolate brown skin as did everyone else he had ever encountered in his life. His hair was black and curly and these people, he saw, had hair of many colours.

One of them had found a stick and was drawing in the sand. He pointed to the sun and drew a circle. then drew a little stick man and pointed to the mountain, then handed Pungo the stick. The man pointed to the sun again and the bewildered look on Pungo's face cleared as he understood. He bent over and drew three circles in the sand then pointed to himself. It had taken three days for him to get there.

This seemed to cause some excitement. They patted Pungo on the back nd started pointing to Pungo and the mountain and then themselves. So he nodded and smiled. That seemed to make them all very happy.

It was beginning to get dark now and a fire was started with wood taken from the surrounding scrub. Blankets were laid out on the sand, boxes were opened and Pungo gazed in wonderment at the strange-looking food. He accepted a chicken leg with a smile and proceeded to devour it in haste. Pungo was, after all, very hungry. It tasted good, although he did wonder what kind of creature it came from. It must have had many legs. he thought, which all the people were eating.

Then they showed him how to open the top of a container and indicated for him to drink the contents. He didn't like the taste but he didn't want to seem ungrateful so he drank it down quickly. He was feeling a little dizzy after that, and very odd for a little while but then felt quite happy as the people began singing and dancing to music, the like of which he had never heard before, which was coming out of a small box.

Pungo was still full of curiosity and the wonder of it all and feeling a little sleepy, but then couldn't help starting to feel apprehensive as he heard voices getting louder and louder. Two of the men started yelling at one another; one was pointing at the rising moon, the other was shaking his head. Then they were pointing at him and the mountain. So Pungo lay on the sand, pretending to sleep. But he knew. He knew what they wanted to do!

Eventually, one by one, they all quietened and fell asleep on the blankets, and Pungo lay still, watching and waiting until he was sure, then he rose up and quickly took two chicken legs which had been left by the dwindling fire, stowed them away in a pouch hidden in his goatskin and softly padded his way up the track he had noticed going around the bottom of the cliff. It led around the hill which he had fallen down, and he hoped it would go back up and would lead him away from this place to his mountain.

During the next three days it took Pungo to retrace his steps and find the tracks which would take him back home, he was lost in thought. He had discovered that the edge of the world was water which stretched away to the stars. That strange people from another land wanted to go with him up the mountain.

He thought of his peaceful happy life with his tribe. He knew no other way; they had kept their existence apart from the outside world for many years; strangers who tried to seek them out were never allowed to leave. Many bones were hidden in caves, as Pungo had once discovered when, full of curiosity, he had followed his father, who went there carrying large sacks.

So Pungo made up his mind. He would tell the story of his adventures and how he had found the great water at the edge of the world and there would be a feast and much praise for his bravery. He decided not to mention the strange white people. No one would believe his story of the water house, and they would say, 'Pungo tells good stories,' and laugh at him.

One day when no one was paying any attention to what he was doing, Pungo made the long walk out to the caves and came to one in particular which he regarded as his own secret place.

He took a sharp rock which was good for carving on stone and went far back into the cave where there was still enough light to see, then all over the walls he made drawings of the water house and the white people and the strange clothes and as much as he could remember. He also included a picture of a small creature from his imagination which had ten legs.

When he had finished, he covered the entrance to the cave with rocks and tree branches and, feeling well pleased with himself, he started the long walk back home.

Shadows

It was very dark on the other side of the road and Jess decided that as long as possible she would stay on this side. Sooner or later she was going to have to cross over, as she would have to go around the corner to get to her street. She considered going back the way she had come, going through the park and out the other side, which would bring her to the other end of her road. But this would be silly, she decided. It would add at least twenty minutes to the time it would take to get home. So she kept walking.

Jess glanced apprehensively across the street, then up at the sky. The sun was sinking low, casting long shadows from the buildings opposite, reaching almost to her side of the road, where there was still some sunshine. Jess was not normally given to fantasies. She was a logical lady who could usually find a reason for everything however odd it seemed at the time. Now, however, she decided she could find no good reason for these feelings of apprehension. She looked around and decided she was being ridiculous.

And then, the slight breeze which had been gently blowing her hair about suddenly stilled. An eerie hush descended, quietening everything around her. There were no traffic noises, no birds. Jess placed a hand over her heart – she could feel it beating fast, and the air of oppression was so strong, she couldn't seem to breathe and she suddenly felt cold in spite of the sun which was still lingering on her side of the street. Jess looked behind her, but there was no one else in sight. She was the only one who had got off at the bus stop and the street was deserted.

She had only moved in to the boarding house last week, then had started today at the new job, so she hadn't had time to really check out the neighbourhood.

Her landlady, Elsie Price, seemed nice enough and had even offered to show her around the local area. She had also given some advice. 'Try to get home before the sun sets,' she had said.

When Jess had asked 'Why?' she had replied that it was safer, then added, 'Stay away from the shadows.'

Jess pondered on this now. It had seemed to be a strange thing for Elsie to say and she was beginning to wish that she hadn't spent so long looking around town before catching the bus.

She glanced across the road again. She couldn't even see the buildings; they were shrouded in shadow. She tried to remember what was there. Was it shops? Or houses? It must be houses, she thought. But why did they look so dark? The sun still hadn't properly set yet.

She was feeling a little spooked now and unaccountably scared. Jess suddenly stopped walking. She had seen something moving that was even darker than the shadowed buildings, just a big black blob. She squinted, straining her eyes.

She could just make out the outline of a very large animal of some sort. It was much bigger than a dog. It definitely had four legs, she thought, and an enormous head with something sticking out of the top. Horns? She shook her head in disbelief. Sometimes, Jess knew, her imagination ran riot. But next, there was no doubt about the two lights coming from where she thought the eyes would be if indeed it was an animal of some kind, and when it stopped still and two bright orbs seemed to be staring straight at her, right across the road, Jess froze in shock. Then, quickly gathering herself together, she looked behind and, seeing a recessed shop door, she slowly backed up and pressed again the window.

She was mostly hidden from view now from the creature and she cautiously peeked around the window. The eyes had disappeared from view but then she watched in amazement as it jumped from the ground with an almighty leap, right up into the air, then disappeared into the darkness.

Just then, the street lights came on. The other side of the road was no longer in darkness, a gentle breeze had sprung up again and she could hear a car revving its motor a short distance away.

Jess stared at the old house across the street which was now visible. It looked as though it was unoccupied, windows broken, garden over-grown and a gate hanging off its hinge, and then she looked up at the roof. Just for a moment, she saw an enormous black figure outlined against the sky, standing upright next to the chimney, just before it leapt off into the night and disappeared from view.

Jess waited a few minutes as the sun set lower and the shadows reached her side of the street, but they no longer felt threatening. The other side of the road was no longer in darkness and the terrifying sense of fear seemed to lift.

So she let her breath out, which she realised she had been holding, and started a slow jog, which was all she could manage until she reached the safe confines of her friendly boarding house.

Elsie was waiting to greet her when Jess arrived, albeit a little puffed. 'Found your way home all right then,' she said with a smile. 'I was get-ting anxious.'

Jess wondered why her new friend seemed so happy to see her and thought it was nice of her to be so concerned. 'Yes,' she said. 'No wor-ries,' and then decided that tomorrow she would perhaps get an earlier bus.